MW01634054

OF FISH AND GAME
AND BUTTERFLIES

French publishing, Ressouvenances, 02600, Cœuvres

"dépôt légal" 03-2022 - isbn 978-2-84505-289-5

Pierre Bergounioux

Of Fish and Game and Butterflies

THE LINE
WOULD-BE HUNTER
CHILDISHNESSES

*Translated from the French
and presented by*

Claude NEUMAN

RESSOUVENANCES

CONTENTS

Pierre Bergounioux

Pierre Bergounioux, writer, sculptor, teacher, was born in 1949 in Brive-la-Gaillarde, in the barren, backward French region of Corrèze.

A prolific author, his works comprise over forty novels or novellas, mostly autobiographical, some thirty essays, often about the nature of writing and recollecting, and a diary kept over the last forty years.

He was struck at a tender age by the fact that the books he was borrowing at the municipal library were all about places and people that had nothing to do with the ones surrounding and baffling him. Those were left unexplained, ignored by literature, history, philosophy and sociology. Yet, stubbornly, he kept looking for clues, and found some in Faulkner, Michelet, Descartes, Bourdieu… and it dawned upon him that his native badlands were a blank on the cultural map because they were too poor to have generated the economic surplus necessary to subsidize a caste not concerned with the production of basic necessities: writers, thinkers, artists inhabited the better lands and their cities. He resolved to give testimony between the covers of his books of a second-class world that had fallen between the cracks of time and was gradually disappearing into the sameness of modernity, and to give voice to its overlooked denizens, as one of his literary heroes had done for those of an obscure county in Mississippi.

The stern, humid, thorny barrens of Corrèze are a borderland, though: a few miles south of Brive lie the fertile Dordogne valley and the sunny plateaus of Quercy. Young Pierre had to grow up on the wrong side of the border and took this injustice personally. His prose evokes nature like few others do, but, depending on location, she can be the object of his homage ("Perhaps Creation would lack something, were we not, holding back our gesture, suspending our course, raising our eyes, granting it in passing that it reigns in all its glory, magnificence, profusion, splendor, infinity.") or of his resentment ("What remains when nothing ever happened? The whims of the relief, the cover, the humdrum activity whose patient setting they supply, the scrawny habitat.") [quotes from *The Line*]

The landscape and society of his badlands didn't offer his young eyes the sources of wonderment he was craving, so he pursued them in their speechless dwellers: "I was born in a desolate, rugged, wooded, wet, underpopulated area. The wild life found it easy to persist, discreetly, in the immediate surroundings of the inhabited places (...) It is because the highly elaborated products of culture were cruelly lacking, on the periphery, that I turned my attention towards nature's masterless possessions".
(https://diacritik.com/2021/03/24/bestiaire-entretien-avec-pierre-bergounioux/)

The three novellas brought together in this volume describe this lifelong compulsion.

Pierre Bergounioux, who won several literary prizes, most recently the "Prix de la langue française", is widely acknowledged as one of the greatest and most original contemporary French writers, his style a unique blend of refinement and brutality. His works have been translated in German, Dutch, Spanish, Portuguese, but never before in English.

Claude NEUMAN
neumanclaude@gmail.com

The Line

It would be delightful to write about pleasures, if by doing so one could impart them to others. Unfortunately, nothing is more difficult than to convey any ſtrong impression of pleasure which has been felt within us.

We do not all care for the same pleasures, and do not want to hear about those of other people.

Lord Grey Of Fallodon, Fly Fishing.

I hate fish.

There exiſts a word for designating the movement that leads us to the pursuit of what we know very well we do not like, though. One speaks of fatality.

Ancient medicine relates the passions of the soul to the entire universe. We play our part, as often poorly as well, at the interseƈtion of the two regiſters, each of them quadruple, of matter: the inner one – the humors – and the one that swirls outside. Here, the mechanics of primitive fluids, the conveƈtion of vital liquors – yellow bile and phlegm, blood and black bile – there, the eternal confliƈt of water and fire, of air and earth, the tumultuous realm of the elements.

If we had our say, it is from earth I would have wished to proceed, to be molded. It is its equanimity, its patience I would have liked to taste for the duration of the border incident that opposes the substances, themselves divided, of within and without. I have, on this point, a certainty as old as the incident itself. An innate, irresistible penchant draws me towards the earth figure which in Hippocrates' time, already, the chisel of the Greeks had conjured out of marble under the name of Cybele.

But no one sought our opinion. What is happening is within the purview of matter, what we think of it of very little importance, secondary, almost, and can change it in no way. We will have been the narrow, fleeting seat of the blind torment that agitates it, and that is all.

I didn't have a chance.

On the paternal side, they were intoxicated with black bile, bitter and scrawny, stubborn, sedentary, continually despairing. On the other, dreams prevailed. It made for thinned out, mobile figures, flung high in the air, imaginative and sunny. In short, the most opposite features, the least compatible beings one can imagine. Of course, it is afterwards that we figure this out, when they have left the outward space and we realize that they are us, that we are them now. We discover that we are bearers, in equal parts, of the antagonistic attributes they were burdened with respectively, with the obligation of putting a semblance of order and unity in the ſtormy assembly we harbor, of pacifying the living Erebus we have become.

Placed as they were under adverse signs, facing, the former, melancholy, the others the spell of a fancy, it is not surprising they sought remedy in water. It assembled them on its banks, purging the small dark ones from bitterness, channelling the dreams of the dazzled lanky beanpoles.

I was seven when grandpa departed – or so he seemed to have. Strangely, the memorics hc left with me are diſtinct from the ones that show me my father in the same times, whereas they often occupied the same image under my eyes, when it was reality. It may be that, already suspecting how much they differed, to what extent it would be difficult to hold them together when I had become them, it is not to be excluded that I took, as early as then, the precaution of separating the images life turns into, of compartmentalizing in advance the house of memories, the residence of the paſt. I have two entries, one showing small characters sitting down, sullen, morose, the other tall figures blurred by light. With two exceptions. The firſt pairs grandpa with his son-in-law, back from fishing, by the thundering motorbike that my father, who didn't care that much for life, which bored him, was ſtill riding when I turned up. I run from the back of the garden to meet them, to see the fish they were to bring back from the river, and they have caught nothing. The second shows them together, with me as a third party, at the water's edge.

So much for the inner space, the Styx running through us.

One chooses outer reality no more than the taste of dreams or the tenebrous philtre. It could have been elsewhere and it was there, on the oblique, rugged zone, itself a border, which separates the Aquitaine plain from the Massif Central, whose granite heart, hermetic to water, rejects it in gullies, in creeks, perspires and dries itself off, feeds peat-lands, produces ponds. The old names are saying nothing else. Millevaches, in the east, is mille aquas – myriads of sources. The Corrèze – Curretia, the coursing one – gallops westwards with a noise of hoofs, agitates its foam manes in the gorges of the metamorphic zone. It hastens towards the Vézère, its sister, whose cradle it shared and then swerved away. It joins her again in the land of the first men, the ones who adorned its banks with horses and mam-moths, with hyenas and bears, with salmons, with signs one finds obscure and that are limpid like the waters, that speak of great hunts, of the legendary sturgeon fishing. The towns themselves, the late enclaves, when not evoking defensive height, the Gaulish vic and dunum, like Neuvic d'Ussel and Le Puy d'Issolud – Uxellodunum – where the Cadurci, in the year 51 (will all due respect to Caesar *), fought and died for the independence of hairy Gaul, the towns speak of the water. Brive, on the Corrèze, and its small double, Brivezac, on the Dordogne, come from the Celtic briva, like today's bridge and Brücke in German. There are the fountains - Bonnefond, Fontfreyde and Les Fontbelles – La Bonde and La Rebeyrotte, Gransaigne and Hautesagne – the marshes - Riousal and Le Rieutort – the streamlets, one of troubled water and the other sinuous - Saint-Cirgues-la-Loutre ("the-Otter"), Fontourcy where drank the aforementioned bears ("ours" in French), Lagane, Ganette and Gasneclaire – the creek, in Gaulish - the Latin Entraygues, and Lafage-sur-Sombre, Laval-sur-Luzège, Lagarde-Enval, Gouttenègre – the black source – and Les-Quatre-Moulins ("Four-Mills"). To which the hand of man added, yesterday, the great dams staggered along the Dordogne: L'Aigle and Le Chastang, Bort-les-Orgues and La Valette, Le Sablier.

*: who deemed the conquest completed with the fall of Alesia in 52.

The innate taste for the earth, for the constancy it shows, for the peace it offers us, the personal penchant, perhaps, that I was imparted – if there exist persons – how to follow it when, within, a flow of black bile, a wind of dreams run through you, in spite of yourself, no matter what you think of it, and the outside is wet with sources, shimmers with ponds? I didn't have a ghost of a chance.

One last thing. That is, the name one bears. One chooses it no more than the humors one is flushed with, than the dripping land one awoke in. The rule was then for the three generations of living beings – if there exist living beings – to roll along on two names. One took, upon arrival, that of the grandfather, since he was going to depart. One became, thereby, one's father's father, and so on, continually. So I found myself apparelled with the first name of the tall beanstalk who, I understood this much later, didn't strictly speaking disappear in my seventh year. He continued on at the place assigned to him for after he had left the transient outer light, and which already bore his name outside his body. He occupies it, now. That's why I'm not certain there exist persons, nor even living beings, just blind dissensions within matter, the inexpiable war of air and fire, the hopeless clash of earth and water. I know full well that grandpa's name designates a solid thing, a foundation, that it supplied the Lord the occasion of a word play*. Only, the first apostle, when he was still called Simon, was fishing on Lake Tiberias and, as the saying goes, the cask forever smells of fish.

*: "Peter ("Petros" in Greek, "Pierre" in French), you are a rock ("petra" in Greek, "pierre" in French), and on this rock I will build my church."

Aside from the sweetish scent they give off, except for the Grayling which exhales, as its erudite name – thymallus – suggests, a fleeting whiff of thyme, and the Wild Trout – Fario - which smells of water cold and pure, that is to say, of nothing at all, fish also repel by the sudden alteration which accompanies their passing into the air, another feature, probably, of the conflict opposing, through various proxies, the powers of the origin. In water, it's slightly differentiated water, faster fleeing, a denser silver in the silvery powdering of the current, very little gold for a very short time, that betrays the trout, it's specks of mica, wisps of algae, gravel inscribed within an ellipse.

That's what fish are, as long as they stay in their element and we in ours and that we look akin, perhaps, in their eyes, to something entirely different, to shadows, to trees, to the changing contour of the clouds, to the passing of the wind.

If we were simply ourselves, without useless, foreign passions, the children of the earth born, according to the learned ones, from humus, the fish would remain in the water and there would be a little less disorder in the universe. But agents or victims, it doesn't matter, of an intempestive fire or a dream, we sometimes are dying to remove them from their element. I never approached in cold blood a source, a puddle, a creek. The least movement in the water stirs my emotions. My father, who is sleeping off his sorrow within me, raises his eyes, livens up. Grandpa leaves the sun-splashed esplanades where towers his tall figure, approaches, leans over. And others with them, that I didn't get to meet but whom they remember and whom it is of no importance that I don't even know they lived. They did. They shared that taste. It passed into the blood, with the stream of bile and the vapor of the dream whose immemorial course runs through us for a moment. They are there, all of them, who wish to bring trouble and affliction within the waters. And that is how fish find themselves exiled in the grass, thrown onto the pebbles.

It lasts for exactly the time that they're seeking to crawl through the tangle of the meadow, that they're cartwheeling on the rocks. For that brief instant, it's solid and lively captured water there, silver and gold palpitating, precious stones, hammered bronze, the most beautiful thing in the world. The moment is free of cruelty. Grandpa was anything but mean. What my father contained that was hurtful and bitter, it was against himself, exclusively, that he turned it. While of course, deeming me, rightfully so, an integral part of what, with good reason, he viewed himself as – the fateful receptacle of melancholy – he liberally lavished it on me. Neither of them had a bloodthirsty, a hunter's soul. They never cast their gazes beyond the lower realms, never considered catching, killing other creatures than the poikilotherm ones, screamless and eyelidless, that are barely thickened water, adorned, streamlined in tapering forms.

The appeal of fishing resides, formally, in the very

short moment when something has left its place to intrude into another while keeping the properties it derived from the former. It all ſtarts with the sudden tear of the surface, when it has bitten and it refuses to draw the consequences, to come to us, on the other side. It makes for a whole ſtory rhythmed by approaches and flights, punctuated by muted flickers and sparkling glows, by reluctances, by surrenders. Sometimes it is cut short, when the fish, if it is one, if it exiſts before materializing in the air, breaks the line or gets rid of the feather flake one had ſtuck in its mouth. But sometimes it comes to fruition and the evil spell immediately ſtarts to take hold.

The quantity of movement one had harnessed dissipates. Then, it's the native riches, the glow of fine metal, the fires that die out. There remains but whitish flesh, dreary, cadaverous, in which rise the dark moirés of corruption and which already smells. I'm not sure to be very cheerful or proud when I bring back these faded, disenchanted, unrecognizable veſtiges, as night falls. Each time, almoſt, that it chases me towards the inhabited places where the lamps are being lit, I think that it's useless and disappointing, that it's over. I won't be caught anymore at the passing water's edge, in time irreparable. As a matter of fact, it's two or three times that I need to wash my hands. The slighteſt smell of fish turns my ſtomach, then. Impossible to absorb food that contains water or has soaked in it, salad, fruits, tomatoes.

I wouldn't be able to drink. I would swallow, if I could, flint, burnt bricks, hot coals. Then I hang out, come what may, the long silk line, the magical bond, and throw myself into nothingness. To the distant voice that would predict, on the brink of sleep, that tomorrow I will do it again, I would answer no. No. And the next day's dusk finds me in water up to my waist, hounding flickers, ellipses, gold.

The weirdness of this occupation, its obscure, eccentric character, I verified on the occasion of the encounters one makes by the water. I'm not saying one doesn't come across normal people there, who simply enjoy a moment of peace or who, lovers of delicate flesh, are baiting their dinner. Unlike the bearers of guns who roam in hordes, escorted by their dogs, and tend to be recruited more from the peasantry, locally, Saint Peter's disciples have come separately from the neighboring town. They work more in services or keep shop, are craftsmen, school teachers, retirees, silent, earnest, and get back, punctual, when supper time approaches.

One doesn't come across many people anymore, then. But those who linger after hours bear to some degree a concern or a torment.

He, for instance, who one day made me a gift of lapwing feathers, he had seen me whereas even the animals, first and foremost the fish, take me for something else, a tree in tadpole state, a little bit of pausing shadow or rain. A roebuck once fell for it, in which, reciprocally, I saw for a long quarter-second a great dog of fire pouncing on me. A low ray, piercing the canopy, had set ablaze its reddish livery. It was in the evening, in places dedicated to its inhabitants, for mysteries we don't have to know about. Midday stages a desert on the heights where the sources have their cradle. One stands on the humped spine of the planet, covered with a tightly woven fleece of short calluna, fern and gorse. The pegmatite of the bedrock, when it shows in the gashes of the trails, has bonelike whitenesses. No bird is painted on the cupola of the sky, of an acid, excessive blue. In the absence of the noise we make, we can sense the frightful abysm of the silence. The unexpected water winds through the creases of the heather. It has the transparency and the hardness of glass. The image we take away is among the ones that most look like nothing. It was by chance, almost, that I was brought back there at another time and it is then no longer the same place at all. The light has lost its sterile, sharp glow, the silence its abyssal depth. The heath has been repopulated. The sources are saying something. The air, one can feel it, is run through by gazes, crisscrossed by breaths. The horned beast, devouring, fire-colored, that had nearly hit me, I contemplated with the attention one gives to what suddenly bursts through the screen of relative safety against which are set the objects, our thoughts.

As for what was walking towards me, behind the gathered drapery of a clump of Douglas pines, under the edge of the woods, on another windless evening as I was in the water, I will never know what it was. It weighed much more than a man, if I go by the cracks of dry wood that revealed its approach, but it had our steady gait and not the discordant rhythm of the great quadrupeds that advance in zones of felled trees. I thought of some gigantic guard of tireless zeal, of very piercing gaze, then of an undetermined and powerful creature, of very keen sense of smell, covered with eyes. It advanced, breaking branches, up to the sort of vitrail or moucharaby the wall of a pine forest composes. I was in good standing with the rule of man. I had my permit on me, the piece of paper, duly stamped, signed, imprinted, that allowed me to stand at that place. It was about the hour that one could have picked on me. Fishing, according to the law, must stop at sunset. The orb of day had long disappeared, and it was precisely for that reason I was there. Because there are two different places there, depending on whether the sterilizing power of the ultraviolet is exerting itself, at noon, or whether shadow is coming out of the earth and the woods, like the sources, with its tribe of fish, of indistinct beasts, of birds whose soundless flight makes one doubt they are real. They seem to be obscurity that is condensing, as the fish appear to be solid water, and no more than them will they survive the return of the sun, the meridian, aseptic glow of its fires. The law, if it could fault me, it was on the sole matter of the hour. I counted on finding some red ray all right, hung in the higheſt branches, a proof of the sun, to show for my defense. And as every second, every ounce of time that separates the desert of the day from the impenetrable – for us – country of the night is pregnant with possibilities, I didn't lift my eyes from the fly that would reveal them. One was looking at me, under the shelter of the wrought, latticed surface of the wood. One was perhaps waiting for me to look up, since broken branches can be a way of introducing oneself. But speech doesn't exiſt for nothing, and I kept my watch over the clear flicker on the ink of the water. Whenever it dissolved, I received a trout in exchange, one of those one only catches in those very rare, borderline moments when the laſt ghoſt of day prowls under the vaults of night.

The regular, ſtern and heavy ſtep went away juſt before I appropriated the laſt one, the moſt beautiful one, and I left right after. I thought a very tall, very corpulent man, with the red badge written THE LAW on the lapel of his jacket, was waiting for me near the road, under the trees, where I had parked. Of course, there was nobody. So, I was left with the bipedal and very weighty, ocellated, indecisive image drawn by the shattering walk in the ſtruĉture of the wood.

It was earlier in the season, end of April or beginning of May. So, I was sitting, my back against a willow tree, looking at the creek, which was empty. A change in the light is not enough for trout to be born out of the water as were once the mice out of heaps of old rags, by spontaneous generation. Another condition must be met. That is, the apparition of a certain insect, of an ephemerid whose existence, as its name suggests, lasts only a day and often less. Barely has it spread out its wings over the surface that the water snatches it, and even after it has soared and thinks it will live, a trout, in a leap that reveals her whole, rises to meet it in its flight. When a hatching breaks out, in the hot days, the creek seems to be boiling.

Spring had been cold, late. The ephemerids were still sleeping in the sheaths of agglutinated twigs and sand in which they are, for a year, white aquatic larvas with brown heads, and fishing was pointless. I raised my head. The guy was standing before me. He may have been double the age I was then, had yellow eyes in a skinny face, a voice that sounded like coming out of an iron box or an echo chamber, about him something furious and gaunt, something scorched, too. He was lugging around an improbable aluminum rod he had put together himself, and painted, to prevent reflections. He was looking at the new, expensive gear I had put down beside me: the fiber cane and the green silk that had cost me, two or three years earlier, my first paycheck and a little bit of the second, the fly hung to the ring provided for that purpose. He asked if he could have a glimpse. His eyes, when he was raising them, were really yellow. And when he was lowering his head to examine the automatic reel, of American make, I could hear his deep breathing. He was working at the uranium quarries. He was filling the holes of the drill with explosive and "it wusn't with what he was given for blowing up pieces of the plateau he could buy himself this". It was all said in the same dark, furious tone, without particular animosity. And next, that the water was too cold. Then, that in a week now, it would be okay.

He made his flies on the spot. He peered into the air until he detected in it a movement, a wing. He carried on him an assortment of feathers and some colored thread, a minute mandrel and pliers with which he would instantly assemble a copy of the intrepid insect risking itself in the steps of the cold season. The fish were rewarding his exactness. He had three, in the wicker basket swinging against the small of his back, whereas I would have sworn one couldn't draw, that day, a single trout out of the creek, for the simple reason the hour hadn't come for them to appear, to exist.

I eventually understood what he meant to tell me. That the grey, black-bodied Palmer I was using without seeing a problem in it was the last thing that could intercede. He let his cat eyes wander off into the milky April clarity in which passed, from time to time, a very specific gnat. His respiration had the cavernous depth the great commotions draw from our chest, like an echo of the dynamite charges he slipped inside the rocks, of their blast. But perhaps it was nothing but the great need for air some skinny and charred men have. He looked again at my costly gear, at my ineffective feather duster. Then he drew a cow-leather case from his thin jacket. He opened it with pious gestures. It was lined with carefully arranged feathers. He took a pinch of them out, which he held out to me. Of lapwing, he said. He picked up his aluminum rod. When I raised my eyes to thank him, he had disappeared.

I don't think grandpa knew how to drive. He had worked on the Paris-Orleans line, then with the French National Rail once the Popular Front had granted it the operation of the previously formed track network. He took the train, for his travels. They went fishing together, my father and he, on the motorbike of time's beginnings, the former leaning over the handlebars, glued to the tank, one with the machine, the other sitting nice and tall on his seat, holding like a candle the English cane of slit bamboo he had bought at the turn of the century and which he used to his last day. Among so many regrets that accompany us, there is a very poignant and tender one. That is, to have come a little too late, to have missed the strange company barrelling full steam ahead in the country and which I would have dearly liked, in whatever form – as a bird, an insect, a shower, an edging tree, a ray – to be witness of. Seeing them both, so different, flung into the wind of speed, of time, towards their common water, that, I'm sure, would have instructed me about the conduct to be held, helped me, when the time came, considerably.

We are of one piece, if indeed we are at all, if there exists anything other than a blind admixture of elements thrown without purpose into chronology, if we add something, a dream, a notion, a will, to the tribulations of matter, to its dissensions. When he was asking the water to rid him of his melancholy by way of the reflection he entrusted it with, to take away the bitter and the black he was bringing to its banks, my father went about it as he did in everything else in his life. He crouched within some shelter of foliage, under a canopy of branches hanging down. He sank into the sedges and one could no longer see him. He seemed to have buried himself inside the earth, to have already absented himself from a world he had received only reluctantly and which, up to his last breath, bothered him. It is this absence, combined with the lustral effect of the river, that returned him to us in the evening, and for a few hours still, pleasant, almost smiling, eminently lovable, as he was, deep down, and as the fateful, irrepressible influence of Saturn he was under wouldn't allow him to be at every moment, as I would have wished.

I had learned two or three tricks by watching him, before he drew shut the door of the thicket, the curtains of foliage that were hiding him from us. But it's not that which I wanted to know, not that way I intended to act. We don't know exactly what we are hoping for, what face, what hand will come and fulfill the longing inhabiting us. But one thing is for sure. We are waiting for something or somebody, from the start, and even before that, perhaps, when the humors, the ingredients, the liquors are swirling in the cauldron of the limbos, are composing the very figure in which we will recognize, when we will be - if indeed we are at all – our property.

I remember having seen grandpa fishing his way, that is to say fly-fishing, once and only once and it was on the Dordogne, when it has left its gorges, when it spreads out and flows in majesty. For me to be there, my father must have swapped the big Zündapp for the Topolino that Simca built after the war, under license, and which, besides having the round, receding shape of mice, also was about their size. I don't know how grandpa managed to insert himself into it, how many times he had to fold up his long carcass in order to lodge it in the cabin. Anyway, we find ourselves, the three of us, around Carennac or Pensac, my father and I on one side, immersed in the vegetation, grandpa in the distance, in shallow water, gesturing wildly with his hexagonal bamboo that looks as incongruous in the open air as a small very precious and delicate piece of furniture one would have brought there inadvertently. I ask my father. I don't recall the answer. But it comes with a smile which I ſtill remember to this day and of which, already then, I underſtood the meaning, the blend of irony and commiseration with which I would soon have, but aimed at me, the occasion to get better acquainted. Then, I'm not too sure anymore what happens, if it ſtarts raining or something else. We leave our neſt of greenery. Grandpa moves out of the open water to meet us. He didn't catch anything. I would never see him catch anything because it's in the following winter he died.

So, it was not he who taught me fly-fishing. His rod, which looked like a rosewood Louis XV pedeſtal table, like an amaranthine lady's writing desk, rotted away in a corner. A dozen years passed before the memory of grandpa approaching in the rain, which his departure left in abeyance, found in reality the extension it was calling for.

If we knew, if the notion of what is happening had been imparted to us along with the physical components we received, I would have found ſtrange the features, and the exiſtence, even, of the one who made active, current, the sole, evanescent image in which I ſtand between my father and grandfather at the water's edge. But that is what doesn't appear in the endowment: only the elements, the humors, the very ancient tropisms we will follow even though we might become conscious that they have moved us since time immemorial and lead to nothing. I didn't find special the face of that friend of my father's who practiced fly-fishing and who imparted to me its rudiments. Supposing one had asked me very insistently if I found anything peculiar about it, I would perhaps have eventually granted that yes, I did. That it made one think of pale leather, finely striated, wrinkled, stretch-marked, of the shagreen some book covers are made of. Of shagreen. That's what I would have told myself if we knew, If I had seen things differently, for what they are. But when they are the first and only ones, why would they surprise us? Therefore, I was never particularly perplexed by André P.'s face. And when I was told, much later, he was in turn about to depart and everything was over.

He wasn't working. He belonged to none of the more or less handy categories to which one tries as one can to assign the passions of one's soul. Sometimes I would come across him in the hours when grown men were absorbed by their professions. He devoted himself to fishing, exclusively. He bred in his attic, in the middle of town, half a dozen roosters that exasperated the neighborhood.

He paid my father a visit one day I was there, for I don't know what manly business, of veterans and Resistance fighters. He was carrying a long hollow metal cylinder covered with foreign stamps – portraits of the Queen of England, as it happened. He was coming down from the post office where he had been advised some parcel was waiting for him. As I was looking at Elizabeth II with curiosity, he unscrewed the tip of the cylinder which exhaled a heady perfume of varnish. Then he turned it upside down cautiously and I thought I had found back the misdirected sort of pedestal table, of marquetry piece I had once in my life seen in grandpa's hands and which made my father smile, under the branches.

He regularly sent his rod to London, to the manufacturer, who replaced the bronze rings worn by the friction of the silk, repaired the ligatures and re-varnished the wood. The whole thing was returned to him with Her Most Gracious Majesty's benign, aloof, multiplied smile. He passed for a sorcerer. If one insisted, he would eventually let known, in a low voice, the astronomical number of trout he had brought back the previous day. He is the one that, staggered, I heard proclaim in an even tone the proud maxim: "a fish seen is a fish caught".

I must have worn on my visage something of the surprise that the two bamboo twigs, polished, freshly varnished, signed − like a master painting, like a piece of furniture − had filled me with. Grandpa was too far away for me to see. I couldn't figure out how one can fish with a pedestal table or a lady's writing desk, to say nothing of the incongruity of that boudoir ornament by the stony, bushy, raspy shores of the river. André P. had no children. He smiled in the maze of crinkles that covered his face like the binding of a book. He said he would show me, one day. He squeezed his small chattel into its case and he left. I waited. Then, since it had been an eternity, two or three years perhaps, I stopped waiting. Men in those days were good at putting off their commitments, at forgetting their promises. Or maybe one was excessively impatient. Or else, it was the fact that three years, when you're fifty, are a mere instant, whereas when you're a third that age, it's three centuries they last.

André P. came to see us unexpectedly in the country, where we were spending the holidays. I had to be patient still, to wait for them to have spoken of the usual things, my father and he, on the terrace, for a lull in the conversation to gently remind our visitor he had said he would show me. The heat was starting to abate with the evening. He stood up. He drew the metal cylinder out of the trunk of his car. He extracted from it the whiff of perfume, then the two bamboo twigs which he fit together. Then he fixed the reel to the heel of the cork handle and he asked me to go place something within a radius of thirty yards. Quickly, I went to nab the water pot on the terrace table. I came back to him. I set off again at full speed, counting, and I placed the pot in the grass, a hundred feet away.

I don't remember whether I was incredulous or not, whether I had an inkling of what was to follow or whether a water pot laid a hundred feet away, that really seemed like a lot, a little bit too much. I stepped aside. André P., out there, heels joined on the withered grass, right arm bent, rod in hand, motionless, was looking at the water pot. After that, I don't know. In my recollection, I mean. Now, I do. But the image has remained intact in my memory, sealed off - and that's good – from the foreign elements, from the late clarifications we import into the hours whose radiant magic stems simply from the fact we didn't know. I had come back about halfway. With the second false throw, the silk came rounding its loop before my eyes, and with the third, which was the real one, its tip placed itself into the pot's water, a hundred feet away.

I can date those holidays precisely because it's immediately afterwards that I found myself miles and miles away, a boarder, in grey overall in grey classrooms, leaning over books all day long, fed on paper. My discovery from the previous summer, then from two years before when one more year had passed within the confined air of the dreary classrooms, I had put it in a safe place, with the firm intention of coming back to it. In fact, it's like the old liquors that cook and steam in the cauldron of heredity. It will come back when the time is right. It's always there. That's the way it is. We don't need to think about it. Thinking about it won't change anything about it. Nevertheless, I thought about it, in the evening especially, when I no longer had it in me to read, when my eyes had enough with printed characters, when the same dead day seemed to spin on itself, and time to stand still.

Then came the hours, the fleeting hours of the twentieth year, the mad, turbulent days in which it seems that we're running after ourselves, that we'll never manage. Barely have we considered what's happening, made ours what those moments make us, that they're already one step ahead of us, and with them our own being which they sweep into trials and obstacles - that stranger we'll have to try to become. This, too, leaves rather powerful memories, but whose charm comes above all from the fact their outer respondent, and the hour it was, have finally vanished, are in the past.

So after that, I had a bit of peace. I even found myself bestowed with a monthly loot that was opening to me the gates of heaven, which had here below a legation at the sign of the local gun store. It also offered faceted rods, rolls of plaited silk and, of course, flies whose names reminded one that, although it was on the shores of ancient Asia Minor man conceived of employing the birds' attire to deceive the fish, it was the English who codified its shape and use - Iron Blue, Brown Palmer, Blue Zulu, Olive Quill, Tup's Indispensable, Coch y Bonddhu, Black Gnat, Cow Dung, Wickham's Fancy, Spent Grey, Willow Fly, Light Cahill,

French Tricolore, Cinnamon Sedge… It still had the price on it, when I started waving the eight and a half-foot long sort of antenna over the neighboring river in the hope of repeating thus the feat of the water pot. I found myself tied up in my tangled silk fallen back heavily in a bundle, as many times as I tried to send it afar, to reach this or that leaf or pebble whose distance I reduced gradually and always in vain. My resentment, my decision to give up counted for no more than the feelings, the thoughts if you wish, that inspire in us the humors whose carriers, whose rattle toys we are. We have a perfect right to say what we think, to declare with an accent of truth, heartfelt, vindictive, that we got it, that we're not going to fall for it again. And we find ourselves the next day at the same point exactly, which in itself is not surprising at all since today is yesterday, since we're nothing but a border incident, a passing annoyance, a little bit of foam on the surface of matter eternal and tumultuous.

Luckily, André P. who was always on holiday got wind, through my father, of my troubles. It was the next evening, at the same spot. I was trying to free myself from the bonds I had knotted myself into, while saying inwardly, and perhaps outwardly too, what I thought and which is devoid of importance, of interest. André P.'s voice reached me, borne by the water. He was standing on the embankment and I wasn't at half course that I started briefing him about the junk I had just bought thoughtlessly. He let me talk, come, hoist myself next to him. He held out his hand. I forgot to speak of his hand. The strangeness of his face attracted the attention. But when you turned your eyes away from it, you were struck by the deformity of his right thumb, of its attachment to the fist. The tendon that's there, thickened by use, made a bump, a vise bulge. He felt the weight of the rod without saying a word, raised his eyes towards the river, executed two or three false throws in order to spread out the silk banner, then, with a single gesture, propelled the fly that was at the end of it thirty yards away. That's how I got started. I was not devoid of zeal. I scrupulously discharged myself of the homework he prescribed me, after the teaching on the field. It consisted in grabbing by the mouth a narrow-necked bottle, which you progressively filled up with water, and in moving it until it hurt, by the sole means of the fist, between ten a.m. and one p.m., which is the operative angle of the throw.

We were supposed, when I would really be competent, to go together on waters known to him, and it didn't come to pass. At first, I didn't have the time. Then, when I could have found some, the weariness of age had taken hold of him. The mystery of that life entirely devoted to fly-fishing, it was not he who imparted it to me, but a third party, in the days when he was hardly seen anymore, when he was about to depart. One event should have enlightened me, though. But it had occurred too early, that one – one may wonder if it will ever be time, if there is a time – and I didn't make the connection. We were in town, my parents and I, and we came across Andre P. Civilities, chitchat. A couple approached, neither old nor young, with the clear eyes, the blond hair, the more or less typical features one attributes to the Germans. They were looking for I don't know what and, in approximate French, asked us their way. And it was, literally, another man, another being buried within his being, a scorching, ancient, overflowing hatred that burst out in André P.'s sorrow, in his voice. He belched out, in German, on the two stunned, frightened tourists, imprecations whose meaning escaped me, as well as their reason. He had joined the Maquis in the dreadful hours in which those who intended to remain free had no refuge anymore but in the chestnut woods. He was caught arms in hand, thrown naked to the German Mastiffs which emasculated him, tore him up, left him for dead in the ferns. Nobody knew how he survived. He probably had no clue himself. He slowly came back to the world, to some kind of life, and the water, which he never left anymore, was cleansing him from the blood, the horror, the heartbreak into which his youth had been hurled. Such was the one who, in the absence of grandpa, passed on to me the rudiments of fly-fishing, the use of the great silk line.

It cost me a further year of misfortunes after the despairs of the beginning, one year of superfluous words and of renunciations followed by oath-breakings before the occult powers deigned to lower their gaze on the awkward gestures I was making towards them with my arm. It was in vain, it seemed, I lavished on them the signs of a deep fervor, of an entire submission. Nothing answered, in the water, no visage in the sky it reflected. It was the words of Simon, when Christ urged him to cast his net into the sea of Galilee once more, his disconsolate accent, that often rose to my lips: "But we have toiled a whole night without catching anything." I wasn't spared the trial of physical perdition. I even shuddered with the great shiver its imminence arouses at the root of our being, at the sources of life.

Fly-fishing means entering the water, running water. When you have detected the fugitive circle a fish on the prowl is drawing afar, in the currents, you have to immerse yourself, approach within proper range and present it with the mock insect of rooster feathers in such a way it cannot doubt it is dealing with reality. That's how I found myself, at the end of the first year, in the middle of the Dordogne, downstream from the bridge of M. I was concentrating all my attention on the limited space where something seemed to be happening, while advancing towards the middle of the river. It can display, at that point, a width of some hundred yards and runs on a bed of pebbles. I should have been on my guard. But we only have two eyes and it's on land we have our foundations, our anchorage. The first wader filled up in one go. I flooded the second in trying to escape and I found myself with the equivalent, on each foot, of the ball and chain convicts were fitted with in penal colonies. That was the first thing. The second – there are strange lingerings within the worst emergencies – was to take my gaze off the very specific spot upon which I held it obstinately fixed, leftwards, and to bring it back in front of me. The vision, when I cautiously revive it and study it at leisure, keeps after twenty-five years its irruptive, uprooting violence. The whole Dordogne was pouncing on me. I found myself grappling with a river, confronted without notice and for real with what neither listens nor pardons – water, the elements, matter unflappable – chased off backwards, with filled-up boots like shackles around my feet. There was one last thing, and that's what arose the terror we bear coiled up in the innermost depths of our being. The pebble pavement on which I was sliding down against my will was dropping towards the ten and twelve-foot deep hollows – the "gours" – in which the Dordogne likes to laze, to doze in a sleep that is but feigned, between its sparkling whimsies. They had recovered there, under my eyes, three or four years earlier, with hooks, the bodies of a family of summer vacationers who trusted its little dips, its babble along pebble beaches.

It's funny. It's that day, disputing the ground yard by yard with the river, that I knew myself in charge of life, that I realized it's a grave thing. When you examine it with a cool head, when you think of it in full safety, it may seem it's the business of matter and not really ours, since our thoughts don't change anything about it, since they're perhaps unrelated to what is, and it, in turn, without power over what we think, over our being, whatever it may be. On the very second I understood what I was walking towards, I felt myself filled with a prodigious gravity, the same exactly as that which submerges us, one day, in front of love, and I was cloaked in it, occupied with it until, imperceptibly, the floor below me rose, and life - forgetfulness, the possibility of thinking about something else, of doing a bit whatever we wish, of dreaming – were returned to me.

There was one way out, only one. It was to gain fifty yards laterally before the Dordogne pushed me back a hundred in its axis, after which it would pass over my head. There was one difficulty. It was the fifteen gallons I had taken on board, the equivalent under the surface of my own weight, three quarters, in truth, of the total mass I was in charge of since I had half my body immersed. It's this that I considered gravely. Water, if it was thinking, could easily have cut me off, applied its effort sideways. But it reasons no more than it pardons. The thrust was exerting itself with the same terrifying inflexibility in the same direction. I was steadily losing ground. I was caught up to my belly, now. But even though I was afraid, I refrained from maneuvering too quickly, from seeking too hastily my salvation, lest I should slip on the pebbles, fall backwards, in which case my fate would be sealed immediately. I had the greatest regard for the second body, the drowned one, which the river had provided me with in order to capture the other. I was very careful. I forbade myself the least slackening when I became conscious that the scuffle might turn to my advantage. I was gaining laterally a little more ground than I was losing vertically. Then I gained some in that plane too. The water coming up to my chest started to recede. Then the rims of the waders came out and I rummaged in their clips with a trembling hand, to pull their flared upper parts down to my knees, to return to the river the liquid double it had augmented me with in order to swallow me whole. Later still, the water was only coming up to my ankles. That's when it again started chattering, playing with weeds and reflections, with wavelets. But gravity only left me after I set foot on the sand, after I sat down, dripping, far from the water's edge, waiting for the long shivers shaking me to subside, for the horror to go back to bed and fall asleep.

A month passed, perhaps, before I came back to the same spot, partly because we forget how much the business transcends the importance we give it, partly because that's where it seemed to me I had detected something in the creases of the water, before discovering it was me they were in the process of shrouding. And also, as it was in July of the previous year I had got started and we were in August, I was entering the second year. I had suffered, despaired, paid tribute to the water, risked the whole stake. I was entitled to count on its attention. I deserved its favor, and indeed it granted it to me.

It was the tail end of the age that began on the banks of the Vézère, the one for which stand witness the vertebras of the great purple salmons and the bone-made harpoon points one exhumes from the shelters in the rock, the stone fish engraved in the night of the caves and the skillful hand, the fingered void blown just above them, of which they were prey. At the surface of the still pure waters, huddled shadows, countless, looking like the wedge shapes of the first scripts, spoke to the eyes, to the heart, the transparent language of the river of Eden since they were, those signs, the thing itself and turned, under the fingers of he who deciphered them somewhat, into fish. The invisible depths swarmed with quivering, dense, apparently inexhaustible life, to which the innocents had access in handfuls. I was still more a child than not when a peasant boy who accompanied me sometimes told me, on the first day of the holidays, that a friend of his uncle or the uncle of a friend, I don't remember anymore, had filled big baskets with certain fish whose name he didn't know and which looked like none of the ones he saw me catch. He would show me the spot. In fact, I knew that stretch of river very well, behind a tangle of young alders whose low branches gave off fragrance under the action of the current and seemed to frenetically draw attention to something under them, whereas the water there didn't appeal to me at all. Which I answered to the kid, in the stale tone one takes at fourteen or fifteen to address someone who is seven or eight, and who, moreover, lives in the country.

I kept exploiting areas that were, for that matter, sufficiently populated, cutting short with a word, a gesture, the repetitions of the straw-haired, clear-eyed small boy whose father, a sharecropper of Polish origin, grew tobacco and corn on the riverside silts. The uncle's friend, or the friend's uncle, went on to fill washtubs, so I was told, then a car trunk, then plastic fertilizer bags retrieved from a field's headland, without making a dent in my conviction. Time passed imperceptibly in the wings of the beautiful day, the same one always, so it looked, that came back onstage every morning to accomplish its glowing destiny. At first trimmed in tender blue, fuzzy, virginal, midday's passion elated, consumed it, very high up over our heads, white, before it went away into the powdery, interminable ochre of dusk. That's why I was invariably surprised, every year, to see mom draw one morning the suitcases out of the cupboard in which she had squeezed them the day before, it seemed to me, and begin the preparations for departure.

A harbinger of things to come mitigated the displeasure of that moment and, deeper down, the sort of congenital infirmity to which, on my own, I found myself reduced -because that's me. Aside from the antecedent figures we have to reckon with when they are in the open, at first, and later still, when it seems they have left this world whereas they never so manifestly inhabited it since they are within, since we now are them, the game included a strictly contemporary character – a cross cousin on my mother's side – to whom I owe more than double what, without him, would have served me as possession, as being, as knowledge. He is said to have been conceived just before me, but wiser, even-tempered, level-headed, he waited in his safe place the end of the term whereas already impatient, anxious in the motherly waters, I landed prematurely on the shores of the outer world where he joined me, punctual, five days later.

The same hand that made the opposites grapple with each other, touched by late remorse, wished perhaps to make up for its negligence. It provided me along the way with a material and simultaneous image in order to lighten a little the weight of the arrears I was born saddled with. It went as far as taking care to place us, Michel and I, as mirrors of each other, him left-handed, reasonable, upright, measured, me right-handed, full of frenzies and comedowns, water exerting upon us a powerful, equanimous influence. Such was the living complement, the judicious help that came and compensated for my dreary inheritance, and I have been conscious of it when everything else was lost in the shadowy, persistent presence of the past.

With one half of yourself clumsy, awkward and vulnerable, with a taste for surrender, with despair's persuasive invite, you're tempted to back off in the face of obstacles and to crouch, to dream that you act instead of doing so, to imagine yourself suffering whereas you would have enjoyed impunity. It's because there had been a misdeal in the limbos' apothecary that I received an outer principle of conduct, an increase of being in order to risk myself on the other side.

Michel used to leave at the end of July, for the South. When we would reunite, early in September, he had grown and I was pregnant with extravagant plans, with chimeras, with bottled-up stories that his return made sonorous, plausible, that often became palpable, effective, thanks to him.

Sometimes we would stand still for a moment, talking fast, but sometimes we would already be running, side by side, and I would explain to him in a short, chopped voice, how we were going to launch a pincer attack on reality. We didn't always succeed. It is together that we endured the first and strangest disappointment I can remember. It takes place in the Bouriane region where we have our common ancestry, that sunny side where those we once were took from the things that were there, from the white stone, from the heat, from the laughing, nourishing exuberance of the land, a taste for life, an aptitude for happiness.

We leave in the nascent day the village pitched on the heights. In the valley flows a river, the Thèze. It's probably the first time that we're allowed to set out to see the world, that we test, on our own, the redoubled strengths each of us received in the guise of the other. We may be eight. We prepared hazel poles the day before. We were given line and slit plumbs which we were recommended, above all, not to swallow, and hooks tailored to our age, very small and golden.

The road plunges into a combe with steep walls, speckled with small oaks and junipers. A spell of I know not what sort already circumvents us. We now and then venture into a timid trot, a burst of gallop, without lessening the feeling of slowness clinging to our steps, the impression that the goal, insidiously, is moving back and that we'll never get there.

We reached the farm of La Remise, which marks the valley's entrance. I don't remember anymore whether we carried on straight ahead and crossed the course of the Thèze, only to realize the water was invisible, buried into the earth, plaited with sedges, or else turned left and took the road to Frayssinet. We were going on the basis, already then, of a memory, of a vision depicting a transparent stream, free and not saturated with silt, grassy and black, quasi-solid. I can still see us, treading less and less fast the roadway which sometimes comes nearer the valley's depths lined with shrub, full of reeds, and sometimes brings us back right against the regularly stratified gash in the limestone plateau. The heat is rising. The first cicada has started crackling in a tree and we feel burdened with gossamer fetters, weakened, entrapped.

I was the first to throw my pole in the ditch. Michel kept his on his shoulder. I continued to follow him although it was well established that the Thèze didn't exist, for us, at the age of eight. We may have had the adults' permission to go and meet it, but the river, for its part, hadn't given its assent. We may be granted to do a certain number of things. These, however, have their say, and in this instance were saying no. I suppose Michel had abandoned his hazel branch too when I gave vent to the dark disposition, to the robust despair coming from the opposite, paternal side. I took an acrid pleasure of I know not what sort in scattering the hooks of gold and the round plumbs in the dryness. We found ourselves empty-handed, motionless, sad, on the overheated road where mirages were multiplying the puddles of fictitious water.

I didn't see then the considerable advantage I retained even in defeat, the beautiful certainty I was conceded in this moment, ſtill: I did exiſt. That was for sure. Michel was looking, talking in my direction. Now, there would have been for him nothing to see, nothing to speak to, on the site I occupied, if, as it was then my intimate conviction, I had loſt not only my gear but the kind of life, as dubious and miserable as might be, that I imagined myself cloaked in at other moments. Left to my own devices, I would have ended up disintegrating in the dazzle, abandoning even the atoms I was made of.

But I unwittingly took note of the lesson of the Thèze, learned that inner resources – or anterior ones, it's the same thing – hadn't been supplied to me in the proportions required by the outer world. Also, that as long as I partnered with the symmetrical complement I had acquired on my way, I had a chance not to necessarily succumb. And even, who could tell? I might prevail. It is from the perdition in which we sank together, in the beginning, that I drew this salutary principle: to wait, each time I was alone. And perhaps did Michel, for his part, poſtpone attempting certain undertakings of which he had conceived the project until the moment I would come and rectify his dissymmetry, support his right side. We have in common a life that combines and surpasses our lives, a country by the waters where each of us is much more than himself, much better than he is.

Two pieces of evidence, among so many, of what I advance, two testimonies of what, as a duo, we were able to wrestle from that which, when separated, instilled fear in us, held us at bay:

The first one, it is from the dead, torpid waters, from the Lethe that can be found away from the currents, that we extorted it on a pearly, motionless, mute August morning in which one had a premonition "already, of incense and toys". *

*: cf. Arthur Rimbaud, "The Illuminations"

A guy we didn't like much was to go fishing with my father, in a rowboat. A late riser, he was still sleeping as we explored the land of mist in which every detail, against all odds, arose in sequence at the center of the circle about ten yards wide that delimited Creation. The distant landmarks that guide us in the plains being abolished, the world's meaning depended on a rock on the path, on a walnut tree whose trunk was of the same ashen grey as the air, on a blade of grass, on a droplet. The river was in its place and the rowboat was rearing its nose out of nothingness. We had the padlock key and very little time, if time still passed in the world we had entered, that looked like a bedroom or a winter tale. The other guy would eventually rise and we would have to yield the boat to him.

I don't recall whether we were following some presentiment or whether it was chance, the magical circle, that arranged everything. We were just the two of us. We didn't talk. There was no need. We were drifting on the heavier, mysterious water, in the subdued silence. At a certain moment we got surrounded by dishevelled shadows. We doubtlessly had crossed the border between the leaden waters, the mudbanks with the spectral alders, the faded air, and the chattering currents on the pebbles, the colors, the sun, the border, too, that's marked by time, by the expanse that separates the hills of summer from the tenebrous gorges in which the year entombs itself.

I may well have bragged, the previous evening at dinner, before the guest, said that we were good at catching fish. But it may have been he, who was extremely full of himself and looked down on everything else, who prompted my boastful words.

Which one of us two detected the oblong shape under the dark water, that's what I've forgotten. We probably spotted it within the same second, Michel and I, and we started rowing hard towards it. We had trouble seeing, but not enough not to figure out what we were dealing with. We looked at each other. Then, we took a circular look at the close-at-hand, timeless screen of the morning reminiscent of Nativity's. What we were about to do, without having exchanged a word about it, was not really allowed. The prohibition was twofold. The use of fish-traps was strictly forbidden in the river and whoever put it there, if he caught us lifting his, would be very angry. As for the find, we thought about it later, when we were no longer busy acting, when we again had the capacity or simply the leisure to think. There were two or three dead fish among the captives. We wouldn't have found them there if the device had been regularly visited. So it had been a while since it was removed by a flood from its initial site and placed in the zone of oblivion where, on an oblivious and grey day, we found it back. We thought we wouldn't extract it from the dead waters, and then it's a living, a glowing treasure of silver bars that we poured into the rowboat. We found the hook that locked the bottom of the fish-trap, plunged our arms up to our shoulders into its overflow of riches, then returned the device to the Lethe, and only then looked again at the day's misty window pane. We got back to shore, further upstream. My father had just arrived, with the other guy who started again, even before we landed, with his airs, his evil tongue and the displeasure it brought. Then the rowboat touched the bank and his fresh little laugh got conjured away, no more, no less than the rest of the universe, by the morning. I had spoken rather carelessly the previous evening at the dinner table, and I had the good sense to keep quiet. Michel, in this matter as in others, proceeded with discernment. We left them the rowboat whose cargo was sparkling, palpitating, and we got back home in the day still new.

It's in the same shifting hours of the end of the holidays that I told Michel what the peasant boy had said to me in the beginning. I didn't conceal from him what little credit I gave it, nor the doubts the spot raised in my mind. I described to him the brutality of the current, the maniacal, tiresome frenzy of the low branches. After which we found ourselves at the spot I had juſt talked about. Water talks, too. When we arrived and Michel saw it, heard it, he sat down at the top of the embankment. I would have done the same had I been him, but there he was and I was me. I went down. The current was coming ſtraight on, of a piece. Over it, the trees were giving off fragrance mechanically. I caſt a dull gaze on the bank, which returned it, threw my line along the wild branches, pulled it back, doing it as in a dream, doing it ſtill, forcefully, without thinking, so convinced was I of the contrary, that I had caught something. I hadn't realized, when a big fish with golden refleċtions burſt through the surface, and – I knew so even before I underſtood I got it – it was the firſt time we were meeting. Michel was already there and it's together that we more or less immobilized it in our four hands in order to examine its cylindrical body, the drooping whiskers on its fleshy lips, the jagged radius of its dorsal fin.

The important detail, we noticed laſt. It hadn't bitten, as they say. I had hooked it right in the head, almoſt between the eyes, on my firſt try. I said so while extraċting the iron from the thick, muscular, convulsing flesh. I added that it was not possible, that for this to have taken place, which yet had just occurred, the water in front of us would have had to be built of, saturated with, made of fish, of big barbels in this case, whereas it presented all the appearances of water, and of the most disappointing kind. Michel threw his line while I watched him, the Gallic fish in hand, perplexed. He immediately met in turn with the brave but disorderly resistance the fighters from Avaricum and Gergovia once opposed to Rome's legions. Then, in a great splash, he drew out my fish's twin and then everything decidedly changed. There was nothing different, nothing more. It was the same fast, rectilinear current, fringed with exhausting alders under the overcast sky, and it didn't correspond anymore to the idea we had of it. Or then, reality was our idea. We only had to imagine that what we craved was there, despite the testimony to the contrary of our eyes and of all things, and that's what would happen.

It wasn't the rain that sent us back home. We were in the water and much too busy, anyway, to care about what was happening in reality or in the idea we had of it and to which the barbels were subscribing. It was the barbels. They formed a stirring heap on the embankment on which we were throwing them. To take them away, we made bags out of our jackets by tying their sleeves together. We marched into the shower. We dropped our booty on the terrace, halfopened the door to say that we just needed big bags, that we were off again. We found ourselves stripped off, like two rabbits, of our drenched clothes, in our underpants. As mom was rubbing our backs, our heads, dressing us in dry raiment, all we were thinking about was the river and our idea. We finally escaped, plunged back into the rain. We were wet down to our marrows before we found back the water, but we had taken flour bags with us. We filled them with big golden, pugnacious, whiskered beasts. We came back and poured them on the terrace. We set off again in other clothes through which the shower filling the afternoon ran once more. I don't remember how many fish the profitable and crazy idea we entertained delivered us. They must have spawned in compact schools to yield to us, each time, a shimmering prey caught any which way, by the belly, the tail, the gills. We satiated the area round with them. But before distributing them in the neighborhood's houses and in the farms, we wanted the illusion or the fact, it amounts to the same, to be attested. It was probably in the order of things or of what, for a fleeting moment, had replaced it, that the cold camera lens and the silver salts couldn't keep a record of it. The print was useless. On the negative, at the bottom, in the foreground, the eye may detect vague dark shapes, lying countless. The rest is lost in night.

I never liked fish, but it's probably at that time, when I often brought back so much of it as to erect living pyramids, scintillating trophies, it's then that I conceived for it this final and violent distaste. Which in no way prevents me from coming back to the edge of the waters to take down their words. I am, and so was my father before me, and grandpa, and going back to the owners of the ghostly hands floating in the painted caves, of the age of which it was said, written, that "its waters would teem with fish and that we would be blessed and would rule over them" [1]. But it was my generation's fate to experience its end, to feel all the rigor of the Fall.

So, it was the second year. Evening was falling on this part of the Dordogne valley I see in halftone upon the day's triumphant entrance, when I read in Genesis the birth of Paradise on Earth. The sun had disappeared behind the riverside groves. Cleared from the brilliants, from the glowing pomp it trims them with, the water, the sky, the rocks that the water polishes with its interminable fingers, the grass and the trees appeared in the moving nudity of their color, which is suave, which it seems you could taste. The river, in that moment, is a foil of matte silver. No breath was dulling its luster, no chase either. It might have been as devoid of soul, of life, as a casting of cooled metal. But it was the second year. I had learned, paid my dues. I got in. The Dordogne was low and barely moved. A child could have bridled it.

There is an expression – "fishing water" – to say

---

[1]. [1] Cf. Genesis 1:28.

that you proceed in the absence of clues, of the circles that betray the fish when it rises to catch an insect on the surface. But with practice, with the solicitude, too, of the elements, of the spirits you have ingratiated yourself with, signs are not necessary. You go straight to the thing, as if by magic. I took out ten yards of silk, by way of a preface. I still had good eyes. The brown, very simple fly – a Willow – stood out so vividly that it seemed touched by a line of light, by the adorable index finger the quilled archangels point. I unreeled ten more yards. The Willow resumed its march under the invisible ray and vanished. The surface wasn't disturbed in the slightest, and it was as if I had just hooked the river.

We were moving no more. I, because if I pulled back in the least, everything would break, the silk, the rod, the infinite serenity of the landscape. As for the Dordogne, I really don't know. We stayed confronting each other, like the previous time, except that it was gaining no advantage on me, nor I on it.

The trout is a complicated lady. It is possible that the three or four thousand volumes that have been partly or totally dedicated to her still give but a very imperfect idea of what she is. Her distrust is legendary. Her energy already "amazeth" Belon who describes her anatomy as early as 1555 in The Nature and Diversity of Fish. One wonders what exactly they are thinking about, those who, page after page, celebrate the rubies of her coat and her princely splendor, her whims, her scorns, her fickleness. A touch of misogyny helps take a saner view of the facts. A somewhat patrician extraction, too, that guards the observer against certain prestiges imported from the social spheres. When these two features are found combined in one and the same individual, Henri de la Blachère for instance, author in the past century of a very good General Fishing Dictionary, one has some chance of encountering under his pen something that resembles reality. He is the only one who considers the trout an inelegant creature, stocky, with heavy head, square tail, fierce look and evil eye. That is indeed what is revealed by the impartial survey of the steel engravings that adorn the natural history books, or of the wicker basket, when it's all over. But between the moment when she keeps, in the water, an image-like immobility and the one when she regains it on a bed of ferns or nettles, there is the turbulent episode during which the trout, if that's indeed what she is, if the word is appropriate, has nothing to do with the beauty in the madrigals and rondelets the anglers like to compose when they take to the pen. It's a liquid explosion, battering-ram blows dealt in all directions, a confusion, a savagery making one fear never to finish her off.

I had a little experience of torn water, of the frenzies you unleash twenty feet away just by lifting your wrist a bit briskly. That's why I was wondering. It was pulling with the regularity of water, with the formidable tenacity you suddenly discover underneath its childish games and its laughs, and which makes you grave, infinitely. I have no idea how long it lasted. The moments evidently carried fragments of the great flow of time. I gained half an inch and it was as if I had forced the Dordogne to turn back upstream by as much. Nothing moved at the place where the line plunged into the water. I committed my first error. I advanced to meet what had caught the fly and wouldn't let go, instead of staying near the shore. The water, as I said, was lazy and low, friendly. The distance started to diminish, but almost only through my own motion. I was wondering what was happening to me. At times, I thought that I had caught the river, that I was trying to wrestle it out of its bed, whole, from mouth to source. Barely was I given back a hand's width when, for my part, I had made a big step forward. There is another expression. They say the fish "whitens" when, as its strength abandons it, it slowly turns on its flank. No such thing occurred. Daylight had much diminished, the river had blackened. We got closer to each other still, without disorder, splash or noise, gravely, like the previous month, when the water was pushing me backwards straight towards its lairs and I was yielding inch by inch, obliquely. We were less than two yards apart when we saw each other.

Of course, it was a very big trout – four pounds, maybe five – of the color of the falling night, that floated under a thin layer of water, at my feet. She might have been there by chance, out of coquetry or bravado, if it wasn't for two equally curious details. She had the minute Willow pinned into her upper lip and I could see the pure, pearly white of her mouth that opened and shut spasmodically. She was probably tired, but not enough to show me her flank. One last detail deserves to be mentioned. She didn't do what all trout try, though spent, exhausted, when they spot their foe – to desperately set off again, to consume in a last fit of frenzy their last strengths. Just as she had merely pulled with the constancy of a river, she was undulating before me, no more, no less than the peaceful water of the evening. I had no landing net. The bank was forty yards away. I committed my second mistake, twice. I took her by the nape of the neck. She wrenched herself free in a single sudden, very fast, offended movement. We are incorrigible. I did it again. Same lightning-quick evasion which had the effect, that one, to make the line snap off on the eye of the fly. She was free now, but she wasn't going away. I was looking at her intently. I could still see her very clearly. I hadn't understood. I didn't want to. It lasted long. It depended on me. This moment could have prolonged itself indefinitely. We would have entered the great flow of time together. The image was already slightly blurred when I held out my hand through the layer of water for the third time. I grazed the big black, rebellious body, and it's only at that moment the trout disappeared, taking with her the Willow which she perhaps simply wished to trim herself with, like the beauties of yore who, in their sitting rooms furnished with pedestal tables and lady's writing desks, used to put a black mole above their lips – Mole Fly. I could see less and less distinctly. Night had come. I was blubbering my eyes out and it just added a bit more water to the water. I waited for it to stop and I got back home.

The same month, the first of the second year, had another disappointment in store for me, or at least the confirmation that it was in the nature of the very ancient things I had thought I would unify, to be adversarial, irreconcilable, and to remain so. My father, who had followed my disastrous trials of the previous year with an amused eye, my father liked, in the afternoon, to moor his rowboat over the depths at the bottom of which I had come within a hair of ending up. When, at the decline of the day, I repaired to the upstream currents, I would discover his figure in the distance, motionless over its reflection. The calm water was taking away the acridness he was saturated with. But he still had enough left to comment at dinner on my little setbacks. And even when he abstained from saying anything, he had that smile I saw on his face the day grandpa, out there, was drawing loops in the air without success.

I had noticed, when, disheartened, I would go

wait for him on the bank, that big white fish were circling round the rowboat near the surface, with impunity since he was fishing the depths. He fished, in fact, less and less. The dark disposition was prevailing, with age. Water no longer had any effect. He was sleeping off the black philtre he had sucked with maternal milk and he probably yearned in secret to find back the indifference, the absence he was wrestled out of without his consent. It was on an afternoon of this kind that I approached him. I asked him to lead me to the bend the river made, because I believed myself able to catch the big daces – vandoises in French, which comes, they say, from the Gaulish vindesa, meaning white – that were strutting about under little water. He gave a hint of the chagrined look, of the annoyed, weary gesture I knew him for, and firmly laid his sad temple on the spread fingers of his hand. But it was the second year. It was like with the big trout, like with the river I had held captive with her for a moment, before losing everything. I was capable. I knew. I stepped up my siege. The pains, the amount of energy needed to break the spell, to drag my father from the desolate solitudes he lived in, if that was living, to the shores of the real world! I eventually extirpated him from the wicker chair. I put the oar in his hands and I hastily gathered my gear, keeping an eye on him all the time. Then we set off side by side, on the dirt path that led to the Dordogne between the corn fields. Ten times,

I had to stop between the stalks murmuring even though there wasn't a breath of air, as if they too were party to this, shared my impatience. My father was dragging his feet, seemed with every step about to turn back, to yield to the call of melancholy. But when he was eventually joining up with me and raising his eyes towards me, I could see in them again the flicker of old, when grandpa was alive. It lasted long. We finally got to untie the rowboat. The weather was fair. Summer lingered in the valley of wonders. I was at the bow, leaning, with half the silk unwound, ready, and the certainty that I was capable. My father, settled in the back, was sculling slowly.

The daces were there. They circled in the sun, displayed indolent fins, thought themselves out of reach, above it all, and showed it with ostentation. We got within range. All was well again, and this time there wouldn't be the least mistake on my part. The fly touched down with the languor seen in tired insects. It disappeared immediately. The reflection of the round fair weather cloud shattered. I turned round towards the back, laughing, as if my father might not have seen. I wanted to talk to him, to tell him. My happiness only lasted the time it took me to turn my head and see him. Of course, he had seen, but his gaze was wandering elsewhere and I'm not certain he cast a glance on the last episodes, when the fish arose from the depths where it had sought its salvation, flapped against the planking, then in the rowboat, where it glistened. With the others, which I snatched at will as they were queuing up, it was the same. I was alone or, if you prefer, divided: joyful, elated, supremely, but, to the same degree, also indifferent, melancholy, upset. I could have filled the boat, transferred in it all the fish of the river, sunk it deep under the weight of this miraculous catch. And the memory of that day is just like the life we have, mixed, its own opposite, made, like it, of the separate lives, of the substances whose inexpiable quarrel agitates it in vain. Anyway, I didn't get time to compromise the rowboat's flotation. The afternoon hadn't yet started to decline when my father said that he was bored, that he wanted to get back. I seized the fish I had hooked, which was casting white flashes in the half-light of the depths. I threw it on the planks and we turned back.

It's in the course of the next winter that a flood took away the rowboat and that my father stopped fishing.

We draw silk loops in the air, we place a fly of rooster feathers on the water, we extract fish from it, and that is not, in truth, what is happening. We are governed, put in motion by some fateful disposition, within; outside, we are the toys of the elements. Otherwise, how to explain that taste which shakes up and overcomes our fugitive penchants and even the worst aversions? Imps bobbing up and down, cast into the great cauldron, we are rolled about by the universal bubbling in spite of what we reckon we want, of what we believe we think. The tragedy is that we suspect so. We alone are not in our place, in peace, but anxious, the scene of dreams, the agents of the passions. We are entitled to ask ourselves what effect has on the issue the pensive mindset we were dispensed. It seems to be reduced to the awareness of its helplessness and of its vanity.

Unless the rivers in the evening's fall, the giant earth about to go to sleep, matter eternal, long themselves for the ability we have to conjure up all that we are not. Perhaps Creation would lack something, were we not, holding back our gesture, suspending our course, raising our eyes, granting it in passing that it reigns in all its glory, magnificence, profusion, splendor, infinity. It is this trembling reflection, such as water engenders, but immaterial, labile and knowing itself to be so, that we add to the landscape. It is within it that the trees and the birds, the clouds, the mountains, water itself, acquire meaning and form and exist. As for the fish to which we hold out fake flies, they are but lures and whatever we may do and say in this regard is deceiving, useless, devoid of the least interest.

Would-Be Hunter

In the remote provinces persisted not so long ago the Neolithic, which was a brief and late episode of the Stone Age. It wasn't sure that the time of the great hunts was over. The beasts were acting as though the game continued. How not to lend oneself to it? Here are a few scenes caught live.

Dreams have the ability to restore the past in its tangible patency. But to enter their "gates of ivory and horn", one must have lost the recollection of the present. There is also hunting or, simply, the encounter with wild beasts. And then, it is not only personal memory that is moved and palpitates but, doubtlessly, the one of our anterior lives in the great flow of time.

A part of our inclinations and obsessions transcends immediate ancestry, the example of the men and women whose sojourn we shared in the warmish light. We took from them almost everything that characterizes us, the prejudices associated with a given condition, a few oddities of which we will become aware late in life or never, some very fleeting facial expressions, some inimitable intonation, some gesture, in passing. But beneath the ranks of those we have known, loved, despised for certain of them, tower in some certain hours faceless and nameless figures, fearsome, other, about whom there can't be any doubt that we are them, that they are us.

Geography is a marginal discipline. It is the science of backward countries, away from the cartage of history. What remains when nothing ever happened? The whims of the relief, the cover, the humdrum activity whose patient setting they supply, the scrawny habitat. I saw the light of day, if one can so speak, in the bristly, bosselated, shadowy zone compressed between blistered Auvergne, blackened by the central fire, and Aquitaine, which is, as its name suggests, the land of water. The old names hung on the landscape acknowledged its hold over life, explained the powerful tropisms Bachelard inventoried in a unique style, highly philosophical and obstinately rustic. The Corrèze, which gave its name to the county, is evidently the coursing water, Brive the Celtic bridge, Brücke, which straddles it as it reaches the plain. It has for sister the Vézère, under which surfaces the Indo-European radical that gave hudor in Greek, Wasser in German, water, wet, whisky, the Russian voda and the diminutive vodka, the small water. Both take their source on the Millevaches plateau which certain philologists make a dubious mix of Gaulish – melo, the mountain – and Latin – vacua, void. It is simpler to assume a homogeneous origin, mille aquas, a myriad of sources, which is verified by the least incursion on those heights sauced with peatlands, plated with ponds, crisscrossed with creeks.

My father, my uncles, the one of my grandfathers I got to know, were anglers. In the absence of serious occupations, of historical cares, such as to change the world or simply oneself, they spent at the water's edge the time they were not giving to work. What to say of the hours we shared, they who belonged body and soul to their small land, I who, although I had no idea of it, was due to leave it? First, the sovereign peace spread on the shores, the never-tired contemplation of the plays of light and anamorphoses water inexhaustibly composes, the blessed stupor it induced, in the end. Each time, when evening came, I asked myself: why go back? It seemed to me I had ceased to exist. I was cleansed of the more or less distinct existence which everywhere else was my lot, of the weariness, the boredom of keeping it up, of the vexation of finding fault in it and not being able to do anything about it. The men who have stood near me, right over their inverted reflection, I suppose they too were asking the river to take away what in their life was constrained and bitter, unexplained. In that moment they were different, without the acrimony, the asperities that have complicated mine. It is then that we shall have been together, rid of our puny and sad peculiarity, alike, floating, fused, in peace.

Water conceals from us its secrets, its guests, behind lying images. The magic of fishing resided in the fact that we could see nothing of what was happening under the surface. It was on the basis of deceiving signs, riverside trees, clouds, birds, that we strove to figure out its secret depths. When we managed to make the appearances of vegetation, of sky, coincide with the hidden world, we would snatch some fish. But such harmony was precarious, temporary. The next moment, the two universes would regain their autonomy. The sun had changed course. The wind covered the pond with ripples. We didn't know anymore, and hence the fish abstained from biting. Finally, there never was anything dark or shady in catching them. Their silvery glow, their cold contact, their mutism were the river's. It was as though we had caught water that had condensed, borrowed a seizable, tapering form instead of fleeing between our fingers. There was no blood either.

One last thing. Fishing was a manly business, exclusively. But our ancestry is composed of women for half of it, and not frequenting the places of masculine sociability constituted by the pubs, the rugby stadium's stands, the veterans' reunions, the political meetings and the rivers' banks didn't make their influence less decisive. In my case, at least. All comprehension, light, patience, kindness came to me from my mother, especially in the sinister hours of adolescence, when you despair of yourself. It is then manifest that you have nothing of value, no quality, no aptitude, no possibility to hang on to. There is nothing left but to kill yourself, to seal with your physical elimination an averred nothingness. You would do so cheerfully, if remained not in the maternal gaze an image which, though not resembling you at all, is supposed to represent you. You will work at trying to conform to it. It is the best you have in you. The same tenderness, the same patience she lavished on me, my mother extended to other reprobates. Wherever we were, when she accompanied us, soon came running stray cats, half-starved dogs, more or less snarly, vicious even, and the next moment they were lying in the grass beside her, casting lovelorn gazes at her or nibbling at her fingers. I saw this a hundred times, and still not so long ago the female dog from a neighboring hamlet's farm would climb through the woods up to the house in which we spend a few weeks in the summer. She would be standing in the shade as I opened the door at dawn, would cast a quick, indifferent gaze at me, and resume her wait until my mother appeared. When I passed by at intervals during the day, I could see them under a linden tree, my mother with her book and the beast at her feet. Then came the end of the holidays. One evening, I drove my mother back home. The next morning, when I opened the door to load the car and leave in turn in the opposite direction, the dog was waiting, lying across the doorstep. I let her know in a natural voice that my mother was no longer there. I could tell her whatever I wanted, usually, she didn't understand a thing of it or didn't care. That morning, she continued to look at me, then, slowly, as in pain, she sat up. For a moment still, she stood before the door, her stare lost in the kitchen cluttered with luggage, then she went away in the clicketing dog claws make on cement, and I lost sight of her.

I am trying to understand. Beings and things, when they are with us, we don't think about them. We have to lose them. Then they only exist through us anymore, and it is in their absence that they impart to us what we didn't see when we were together, their true features, their virtues and their flaws, their finitude and also, beyond that, confusedly, the generic entity whose partial, perishable carrier each of us is.

So, as for the men, benign, contemplative dispositions that led them by the water. On the maternal side, this deep compassion I was extended, along with flee-infested mongrels and circumspect cats. In none of them whom I have known, the ominous, declared taste for hunting. It must hark back to times long gone whose hold exerts itself on our transient person and its brief season, all the more forcibly as we have no idea of it.

The precocious, passionate attention that insects inspire in me is probably its perverse, infantile version. For want of being able to test ourselves against big game, we go after prey whose size, discernment and strength are proportionate with ours, in early childhood. I keep present in mind a scene anterior to the autumn of my sixth year since it includes grandpa and he was to leave us in the winter. We are in the public garden, near the post office, him on a bench with a newspaper, me patrolling along the raked sand lanes, between the rosebushes of May. I have put my hands on a golden rose chafer and I ask myself how to kill it without squashing it, because nothing is so beautiful as its emerald-green, very finely nielloed carapace. And at the same time, these death thoughts are accompanied by an intense shame. They must have been written legibly on my face, so that I didn't ask grandpa how to deprive my prisoner of life, and sadly set it free. But I got a rain check. Another fascination, of an intermediate sort, was that exerted by a moth of diurnal mores, the Morosphinx, also called Hummingbird Hawk or Sparrow Sphinx - Macroglossum Stellatarum – which to myself I had christened Daredefil, for two reasons. One was the long filament it unfurled in stationary flight over the flowers and plunged into their calyx. The other was of a subjective kind. It never alighted. It would suddenly materialize right over a geranium or a zinnia, and remain for the space of a few seconds at the center of the brownish halo of its vibrating wings whose drone I could hear. I would approach it with infinite cautions, think I had seized it with the swiftest gesture I was capable of, and each time realize it didn't lie between my clenched fingers. It now hovered over the neighboring flower, in the same quivering immobility, careless of the focused, attentive evil death I was the agent of. I would repeat. It would escape once more with the same suddenness with which it had appeared to me in the garden from which grandpa's decease was to expel me with no return, the following year.

The winter's harshness made it memorable. But I remember the concern that overwhelmed me already in autumn, on the day when, back from school, at noon, I found the house empty. My father arrived right behind me and explained to me that grandpa was not well, that mom was with him. I don't recall whether I announced to him that I was off to join her or whether, as I was to do more and more often, later, despairing of making him understand that I have my own cares, my reasons, I acted without informing him of my intentions. It was a clear and cool October day. The streets, at that time, were deserted. I took the ritual route, crossed the first boulevard, went past the post office. I had reached the site of two particularly depressing buildings that increased my sadness, an antiquated Catholic private school on the right, on the left an old gymnasium with black walls of slate slabs, when I spotted mom coming in the opposite direction. She too was sad, then she saw me, smiled at me, and all my sorrow was gone. It must have happened again, that she wasn't there as I came back from school, but the first day has absorbed the memory of those that followed, until the dazzling, icy one in February when my father announced to me grandpa's decease. I can no longer remember whether it was before or after that moment that came the peak of the cold spell which hit Europe. The thermometer hanging outside the window went down so low that it passed beyond the negative graduation. Three facts remain with me. The river was petrified in ice. Some blowhards had found nothing smarter to do than go down on this skating rink for a car gymkhana. I would witness their ballet, one evening at dusk, downstream from the main bridge. One morning, as we were getting into the classroom, a few of us discovered that our white porcelain inkpots had broken around the small violet mushroom of the frozen ink. Finally, I had collected three birds, a coal tit in the neighboring street, a blackbird on the patch of land adjoining to the leisure house a friend of my father's owns near the Vézère, and then a creature so beautiful that I thought no one had ever seen it. Otherwise, the world would have been informed of it. They would have talked about it. Itinerant exhibitions would have proposed it to the curiosity of the populations, as was then done, not only with the African fauna the circuses presented along with clown acts and acrobatic tricks, but with sea monsters, too. That's how I had discovered, on the long tarp-covered trailer of a truck, a giant Basking or Whale shark, and I can still feel how, before getting in, I was torn between impatience and the fear of being eaten up.

My bird displayed a broad apricot plastron, an azure back, a black skullcap, midnight blue wings striated with white. I knew, as I spotted it on the frosted grass of the public garden that had already given me the rose chafer, that it was victim of the spell that struck the river, my inkpot, its two congeners, and that, against all expectations, I would be able to take hold of it. Which I did in a daze, with the apprehension left in me by the apparitions in dreams and the Morosphinx, of finding nothing in my hand when I would look. It didn't arouse the slightly delirious admiration I had imagined, when I brought it back. After two or three days, it had to be disposed of because, in spite of its splendor, it smelled. Time passed. It's ten or fifteen years later that, unexpectedly musing about the winter that gifted me birds but took grandpa from us, I pronounced its name, almost without thinking about it. "It was a bullfinch."

Like the sulfur-coated tit and the yellow-beaked blackbird, it belonged to the colorful, benign, pretty universe of childhood. But the serious stuff, the great beſtiary was not so far away. The rugged relief, the fundamental indigence of the soil limited the towns' development. Lacking the resources provided by extensive grain farming, by vine-growing, by heavy induſtry, by long-diſtance trade, by political authority, or by the vicinity of a disputed border, they barely reached two or three dozen thousand inhabitants, and moreover came up againſt the narrow walls of the valley wherein they were born. Tulle only owed to its median position its elevation to the dignity of prefecture, whereas it was ſtrangled within its gorge of dark, ever dripping rocks. Brive, further downſtream, benefitted from the untightening of the passage, but it was surrounded with reddish sandſtone heights and had no opening but to the weſt, where the Corrèze and the Vézère, united, subdued, lazily maundered towards neighboring Perigord.

From the tenacious proximity of old nature, of fallow land, of cheſtnut copse, came to me two signs of wild life, the firſt direct, as incredible as the emerald insect and the glowing winter bird, the second legendary ſtricto sensu, in that it required to be read and meditated upon.

A small calico factory had opened at the end of the 18th century, recessed from the river. A canal was dug in order to convey the motive power of water up to the machines. It led to the Theatre's square, through which it ran underground, came out on the other side, then turned twice at a right angle to regain a rectilinear course which brought it back to the river, under the main bridge where I had seen a ballet of cars on the ice of 1956. When I think about it today, the world - that is to say: that which happens, according to Wittgenstein whom I hadn't read - was held within a circle of about five hundred yards radius. Among the great waking dreams of that time comes in good rank that of following the shallow water, in the night permanently installed under the theatre. It was not to come true. At the beginning of the seventies the mayor's office had the canal filled in, that used to take the envoys of the water and the woods to the heart of the city.

I rarely went anywhere in a straight line. The reason, as I said, was that certain places were wounding my soul without my being able to fight it off or even discern the precise nature of the blow they dealt me, the exact part of me they wronged. These are things you feel, intensely, and which, for want of understanding them, you may at least steer clear of. That's why I had figured a range of dodging routes that enabled me to go where my petty business was calling me without having to pay my tribute of aggravation, of distress sometimes, to the evil powers that ruled over a given street section, some backyards, certain districts. To these paths of evasion were added no less than three itineraries of mirth and liberation of which I haven't taken full advantage because they serviced none of the places where, as ill luck would have it, I had business. One was the cramped, complicated maze of alleys, of wee gardens, of footbridges that accompanied the canal up to its outlet. The passage, at times, was reduced to a narrow cemented berm. That's where I caught sight, under very little water, of big bronze-colored motionless carps. They were so close I could have stroked them. I could see their mouths open and close, like ours when we speak, and I may have thought for a while that if it weren't for the water muffling them, their words would reach us, as they once did King Solomon, and many things would get explained. It's less than a hundred yards downstream, just before the canal's mouth, that I saw the bird. The place, for long flood-prone, had just been drained and built upon. A dead-end street, still sprinkled with gravel, was running through it. It bumped against a low wall behind which flowed the canal. Some relatives had just moved into a new house, close by. My first care was to go have a look at the water. I expected to catch sight of the fish, to catch ear of the inaudible sentences modulated by their fleshy and pale lips. So I leaned with infinite precautions over the wall. A brown dappled bird was pacing up and down the mud, right close to me, with composed slowness, and what made me stare was its incredible, disproportionate beak. I looked at it for a long time, my eyes agog, as did Michel Strogoff at Creation before vile Ogarev's white-hot saber blinded him. The chill that had gifted me its pied, child-like congeners was out of season. I knew that if I moved, the woodcock or curlew or water rail would fly off. In the end, I backed up step by step and returned to the house where they were having, I think, a housewarming party. I kept the story of the encounter to myself. It wouldn't have aroused, as I was beginning to understand, any echo among people impervious to the call of the old ages, excommunicated from the enduring mystery residing a few steps away from the brand-new living-dining room where white wine was being uncorked. Such was the first encounter with game, true game.

But already before that day, as soon as I could read, in truth, I had a chance to take cognizance of the open intrusions it was still prone to. The intersection of Toulzac Street and the circular boulevard was occupied on the right by a shirtmaker's shop with a disconcerting sign: The Boar's Place. A slab set into the sidewalk, at a slight angle from the door, mentioned: "Entrance of the boar", and the date, some day in 1927. I've been told that, from the moment I mastered the alphabet, the least outing turned into a nightmare. No way to tear me away from the laborious deciphering of the inscriptions molded into the manhole covers – Puydebois Smelting Works has remained with me – or painted on small enamelled sheet metal placards stuck into the grass of the park. They stipulated that walking on the grass was forbidden, that dogs had to be held on a leash and papers thrown in the "ad hoc" bins. They say I was dumb-founded. Impossible to drag me off. I was stuck on "ad hoc". There was a mistake or else, contrary to what I had believed, writing continued to escape me. Someone who knew no better than I declared it was in American, and I grudgingly consented to move on. So, some twenty years before I arrived, a big soli-tary boar had risked itself into the heart of the city. What a commotion, I thought, must its intrusion within the realm of elegance and trade have stirred, before the police hurriedly came to "dispatch it", in the term of art, with a pistol, in an indescribable con-fusion of silk and lawn. The impression such discov-ery left in me, they must have felt it alright at the time of the event, that they reckoned its memory had to be engraved in marble.

This still, about the imprint you receive, about the fatality of geography when you have not awakened to history, to movement, to reality, to the present. For long, as far as we were concerned, the legend was restricted to the boar's slab on the boulevard, and to a plaque screwed into the façade of the house, in a small street, where Marcel P., Resistance fighter, killed in Mauthausen in 1944, had seen the light of day. So, among the subjects of wonder I was struck by, when I transported myself to Paris at the age of twenty, stands the pervasive text with which almost every wall is historiated, in certain boroughs. For inſtance, near my workplace, a very fine town house bears two by itself. It saw the birth of Manet and Lyautey retired there after having augmented the French Empire with Morocco. Thirty ſteps farther, in a perpendicular ſtreet, two other contiguous plaques signal to the naïve, to the provincial, that Oscar Wilde drew his laſt breath upſtairs and that Jorge Luis Borges used to ſtay there when sojourning in Paris. A Parisian lad, after having deciphered these glowing names, will leave, when the time comes, for the conqueſt of faraway lands, will "wear out deserts", as Borges wrote, or else will risk himself into the scarcely less perilous country that opens out between the cover boards of books. But we, relegated on the humid, bushy marches of the world, were juſt incited to smelt manhole covers or to hound the wild beaſts which were ſtill vying with us for the turf.

It was the woodcock that reaĉtivated the fierce atavism of which had loſt memory the two generations that form, along with ours, the thin fringe of the living, and which, needing no words, the radiant, more than human kindness of the maternal heart was combatting. I wasn't going to wait for a cold spell such as occurs once a century to gift me the creatures whose capture, for want of anything better, was all my joy in those days. I would take hold of them by my own means, and the moſt appropriate was a gun. The years of our beginnings are more made of hope and expeĉtations, of chimeras, extravagances and waking dreams than of reality, especially in the remote, self-sufficient zones which the circulation of goods, of thoughts, has barely grazed. Proof of which was, besides the absence of plaques mentioning that painters, marshals, presidents, writers – French, but also foreign – had ennobled the walls alongside which we walked, the divorce between the life we led and that depicted in books, the ones that reached us. It was an invariable rule that they spoke of places we didn't know, where we had never set foot, whereas that in which our days were spent had never found an echo in the printed volumes. Such was the case in classic literature, in the stories composed by people who seemingly could only write, breathe, live and die in Paris, and whose works evoked locations I never knew what coefficient of realty to credit with. Still, I had at least had under my eyes some engravings or photographs showing Notre-Dame de Paris, the Louvre, the Samaritainc, and I was able to superimpose upon them the adventures of Quasimodo, of d'Artagnan, and Zola's novel about department stores. But I wasn't sure there existed a cemetery by the weird name of Père-Lachaise, so that I was at a loss to stage the scene in which one sees Rastignac challenging Paris on the grave of poor Goriot, just as I couldn't picture the Luxembourg Gardens where ends a novel by William Faulkner titled Sanctuary, which had fallen into my hands by the merest of chances and of which I had understood absolutely nothing. So it was between the enamelled sheet metal placard and the patch of lawn where I had picked up the bullfinch that I set Temple Drake looking at herself in her powder case.

It was, by contrast, rather simple to give substance in one's mind to the hunting tales of which an old collection was gathering dust on a shelf in the backroom of the town library, where the books no one ever consulted or asked for were piling up. This is how I read, alone, the Frenchman Edouard Foa, the Englishmen who gave the Big Game its titles of nobility, Marcus Daly, Rawson Malet, Samuel Baker, above all J.A. Hunter, of predestined name, and Jim Corbett, the subtle stalker of man-eating tigers, my two favorites. They are the ones who, in the absence of close at hand examples, enlightened me on this penchant I had, even though, in keeping with the gap between the situation that was ours and the content of the printed treatises, it wasn't the benign fauna that roamed the area and occasionally ransacked the shirtmakers' shops they were evoking, but the Big Five, exclusively. They are, in this order - but the ranking is subject to controversy – the leopard, the buffalo, the lion, the elephant and the rhinoceros. Since it is Africa that supplied its frame of reference to the Great Hunt, the tiger didn't appear on the prize list. But also to be found under the dust, in the desert of the backroom, was Kenneth Anderson's The Call of the Man-Eater, which is set in India, and the book by Nicolas Baïkov, who was hounding tigers in Manchuria.

When do we eventually enter the clarity of our own consciousness? When we are around eleven, later, never? Yet, one day I faced the facts. To the taste for water and for its guests, which I shared with my male relatives on both sides, I was conjoining the one for the woods, for the warm-blooded beasts, which had, as it were, passed over their heads to strike me in the heart. To the array of fishing rods we squeezed in a corner of the landing, on the first floor, I needed to add a gun. My father kept punctilious double-entry accounts in which the least asset was indexed on a liability. But the transaction was governed by a rigorous loyalty, the contract terms scrupulously observed. When, two years in advance, I announced in a quivering, restrained voice that my reward, once I had passed my first exam, was to be a rifle, I elicited – I was expecting so – a remark devoid of amenity on my chances of success. But when the two years had passed, the ink hadn't dried on the admission list that the rifle was delivered into my very hands, with a touch of solemnity.

Is there a point dwelling on the feats, the crimes it enabled me to commit? It will have been the means to approach, to contemplate at leisure, to my fill, that which we half see, glowing, and from which our heavy and slow condition keeps us separated. The main villainies, which are also the first, I all perpetrated at the extreme limit of range. As with the squirrel shot down two days after I received the rifle, in the bed of the creek that connects an abyssal hollow with the Dordogne, and which summer dries up. One can follow its course up its sandy, sinuous trench, under a cradle of branches hanging down. There reigns an eternal half-light, a beneficent cool, a restrained, almost audible silence, while the sun, glistening, strikes the corn and tobacco fields all round and the elevations of the limestone plateau, of bone-like whiteness. Here and there, deep puddles, the green, the blue seen in poisons, in philtres. Anything can arise in this momentarily out-of-water passage, whose ground is strewn with fragments of colored, polished glass, with fresh-water cockleshells, with iron scraps, with frightening faces, as of decomposed nightmare creatures that had the rest of their body buried under the mud. I recall, when I caught sight of this charnel of intermediary beings, with pig snouts, with big circular lemur eyes, I recall having squeezed the wood of the gun's butt. I was asking myself, as Watson when the hound of the Baskervilles, hemmed with flames, arises from the nocturnal fog, if they would be vulnerable to bullets. Because the foundations of reality and common patency were suspended when one went down into this gallery. The least noise was disproportionally amplified in there. As I couldn't see a thing, the rustle I was hearing ahead might have come from a bird, a rat, but also - why not, in such a place – from a creature whose image was conjured up by that sort of sepulcher, a little downſtream – old gas masks thrown in the creek –. What increased my confusion was that the noise was coming alternately from the ground of the embankment concealed from me by its extra elevation, and from the indiſtinct treetops. I was holding my breath. But I feared that my heartbeat, reverberated by the walls of the trench, by the vault of the canopy, might alert what was approaching by way of land, then by way of air, taking its time. I had shouldered the rifle. The whole world disappears, then, except for the limited, extremely clear space the gunsight carves, wherever it points, in its little tunnel at the end of the barrel. The noise had come closer ſtill, then it had ſtopped. Some sign muſt yet have come to me from the surrounding nothingness, since I slightly moved the aiming circle. The animal entered it. It was ſtanding on its hind legs, immobile, so far away that the gunsight, when they coincided, covered it whole. For that one, and for that one only, I have the excuse that I didn't know. Fish, as I said, are cold, mute, their eyes expressionless and eyelidless. They don't bleed. As for inseĉts, their forms, colors, contaĉt and movements are those of small very sophiſticated, lovingly painted toys, of tiny automatons. When one draws them, in winter, out of the felled, more or less worm-eaten tree trunks in which they have sought refuge, they are numb to the point of remaining motionless when light suddenly touches them. One has the impression not so much of hounding living beings, particularly not beetles, as of stealing gems or gold coins from the cracked safes of the wood.

Nothing had prepared me for the bloody death I was to dispense. I couldn't see my target. The squirrel made a prodigious leap up, then fell back on the sand, where it moved no more. I couldn't believe it was at my disposal. I now dearly wish I had never fired. But I also know, I can recall, of what deep infirmity I was instantly cleansed, what deprivation, what misery, what congenital ignorance were swept away all at once. When I held out my hand to seize the little body, it was as in a dream or as when the winter of childhood had congealed the river, broken our inkpots, pinned the birds to the ground. But it was different, too. The corpse was warm, sticky with blood. I had it all over my fingers. That's when I took the measure of what I had done, as I discovered the wound, right in the heart. The passage of time doesn't explain why I'm missing the recollection of what followed. I have much older memories whose sequence I remember integrally. I may have brought my prey back to the holiday house. If such has been the case, it was – believe it or not – because I supposed one was curious, as much as I, about the secret life that had that mysterious corridor for its stage. What tends to make me think I didn't is that I don't recall my killings causing grief to my mother. But it's not to be excluded that I pained her, and that I rid myself of the remorse by forgetting.

One thing's for sure. The next few days I only fired at cans or newspapers anymore. I went fishing with my father, in a rowboat. That's when I understood that drawing fish out of the water by the lip and shooting down warm-blooded beasts were two distinct, incommensurable passions.

Other than small game like thrush, blackbird, starling, pigeon, I was chasing birds whose color or form struck the attention. They would have gladly done without it. They just wanted to live, to flee away from the violent curiosity they had awakened, and for my part I was deploying treasures of patience and ingenuity in approaching them. One day that my father had declared himself doleful, depressed, and had refused to set off on the water, whereas it would have purged him of the dark disposition he had received in excess, I went down to the river without him. While the fauna of the buried gallery was mysterious, that of the riverside terraces borrowed from the glow of the sun, from the exuberance of the crops, of the vineyards, of the orchards. You had the multicolored goldfinch flights scurrying out of the walnut trees, the pied chaffinches, the jay whose wings seem dipped in the blue of the sky, and then, that afternoon, the scarlet flicker of the bird passing over my head with a chuckle and perching itself atop a poplar. It might have been a game. It was climbing, in a spiral, the top part of the trunk, showing itself for a brief moment, of the same insolent red, only to vanish the next instant. It would soon reach the crest and resume its undulating, sardonic flight, if I didn't act. The distance was such that, once again, the gunsight covered it whole. It fell down in a swirl, its wings half open, which were black, dappled with white. I didn't even think of bringing it back. Of that, I'm sure. But I had to wait for the end of the holidays to look it up in the big six-volume dictionary, with the hope of not finding it. It was there, with its cardinal's biretta, its strong pointed beak. It was the Great Spotted Woodpecker. I had thought, as with the bullfinch, though to a lesser degree, that being so beautiful, and hence distrustful, quick, hard to catch, no one before me had contemplated it at discretion. But of course, to that end, I had to kill it.

Another three years went by. I left my small homeland for a faraway boarding school, and reality migrated between the cover boards of books, wherein it has remained. I don't know why I later made the acquisition of a small hunting gun, then of a 12-bore one, while it was a closed case that the life I had first envisaged, by the water, in the woods, was to go by without me. Perhaps we're still all those we were day after day, and also in our anterior lives. They entrusted us to complete what the circumstances were hindering. Even as we've changed location, views, interests, we hear their voices. As when one of their thoughts comes to us, when we half-make one of their gestures with our hand, when their shadow covers us, like the gunsight of the small rifle as it masked the target. Nothing is lost, nothing dies. This is how I would explain to myself the purchase of an arsenal that was left to rust.

Lastly, two anecdotes, two facts that aim, forgive the word, at redeeming the nefarious acts I have reported. The first is enlarged by the riflescope that sets, as if standing five yards away from me, a splendid old roebuck in a wood's clearing. It wears its winter livery, of a brown at once matte and luminous. It seems to emit a shine, in the faded, shabby copse of autumn. Ah, but if you take your eyes off it for a second, it evaporates. There remain but dead leaves, dry grass, humus, until an invisible finger, an inner or outer one, you don't know, draws again its graceful contour, then places, with infalliblc touch, its beautiful dark eye and its hindquarters' white mark – the "rump patch", in venery terms. I slid the reticle down to the chink in the shoulder, where the heart beats, where the coat lightens, before slowly lowering the barrel. What sufferings come as the price of the extreme contentment one draws from watching up close, from touching, from killing, I didn't know. I learned it, at least in part. It was as if a giant had lashed my loins with his cudgel, or if I had been shot in the back: a throbbing, breathtaking, screaming pain. I had to lie down on the inclement litter of dead branches, of husks, of withered ferns, the time it took for the dreadful poisons one secretes on such occasions, and which had found no outlet since I hadn't fired, to get fractionated, neutralized.

The last encounter is more platonic still. It harks back to the beginning. It combines the ingredients of the legend, the inhabited places, a big boar, but not the engraved plaque signalling its passing, in the past, since it is there and so am I. I'm hanging out the wash, behind the house, which adjoins common woods, in late afternoon. A rustle occurs and the thick bramble bush, right near me, opens up for an enormous black beast – the word came out by itself, in a whisper – that stops still ten steps away from me, as I'm holding a wet shirt in one hand and the clothespin in the other. The animal casts a gaze at me, marks a pause, then, deeming me harmless, negligible, starts trotting on the little hooves that give it the gait of a ballerina, but one that, in lieu of a slender body haloed with white taffeta, would be encumbered with a heavy wedge-shaped carcass, spiked with long rough hair and equipped, to boot, with a pair of strong lower tusks grinding against the upper ones. I thought that my visitor was to vanish as suddenly as it arose, that the interstitial, lateral or dreamt-of time that puts us back in the presence of the beasts had already gone by. Not at all. It was prancing on points around the thicket, was resuming its dance, and I made the same observation as with the roebuck I had, that one, held at gunpoint before letting it go. This very creature of an intense black, as inked or carved out of night, would adopt, the next moment, the dull shade of the undergrowth. The couple hundred pounds of muscles it at least weighed had vanished. Then, my eyes, which were somewhat haphazardly projecting forth its wild form, would see it fill itself out a little farther away, busy, comical, obstinate.

The animal rummaged around under my nose for a quarter of an hour. I thought it would withdraw in the brambles and we would spend the night a few steps from each other, in peace. But something was not to its liking. It growled, then unhurriedly disappeared into the undergrowth. That's it.

We can take the wrong turn. When we realize it, it's generally too late to go back to the bifurcation and choose the future assigned to us by an innate penchant, by the deep voice of the great past. They had no effect because the present, after having tarried beyond measure, eventually reached us and we followed it afar. The beasts whose residence I had shared, whose enchanted path I had crossed at times, have remained for their part in the land of childhood. Perhaps they're waiting for me, just as I now and then dream I meet them again. It will be for another life. I don't know.

Childishnesses

One couldn't rely on the adults. From my sixth year onwards, from my sixth month maybe, I held null and void their opinions, injunctions, prognostications, admonitions. But I also was conscious of my mind's infirmity. As a result, trusting neither my precursors nor the small character whose fate I was sharing by force of circumstance, those years that could have been harmonious, bathed in patency, happy, were full of reservations and vexations, of animosity, anxious, tense, tormented.

It wasn't in the material conditions of life that I was finding fault. I have wanted for nothing. No, what I longed to have, to know, exhibited a quality of weirdness that, consistent with myself, I attributed to a certain unreasonable, deplorable disposition I had inexplicably received.

Among other precocious whims, the insects, whose forms, meticulous details, colors, strange mores couldn't fail to draw, to retain the attention, mine at least. The return of the fine season was always a feast, because it brought back the faithful little winged, painted, myſterious beings decorating grandpa's vegetable garden, on the already semi-rural heights of town, but also the public garden, on both sides of the main poſt office. When I was five, not knowing how to deprive it of movement, of life without damaging it, I captured, then released a golden rose chafer I had caught in the roses, under the ſtatue of a ſtone lady bowing on her plinth, pinching the lower extremities of her dress. At grandpa's place, I snatched a lot of Colorado beetles, of cockchafers, of pierids, the Wall Brown, various types of arguses, the Scarce Copper and the Brown, but the much rarer great swallowtails, the Common Yellow, the Iberian Scarce, as well as the Sparrow Sphinx always evaded me, being much too faſt, too luxurious for me.

The latter's way of flying, in a zig-zag, with alternating ſtationary episodes and lightning-quick evasions, powerfully contributed in ſtructuring my conception of reality. The world was a dull entity, with a dominance of greyish brown, populated with slow people who borrowed from the ambient drabness. What they were doing was devoid of intereſt, of appeal, their words likewise, and come the moment, having aged, grown up, I couldn't see myself imitating them. But I had time. I would decide when it came, if it ever did. Meanwhile, the uniform, tedious milieu was spiced up, crisscrossed with glowing creatures whose apparition, whose possession conſtituted an antidote to the boredom inspired in me by the place, the people, the moments. But living seemed to be inherently complicated. The tiny creatures whose company appeared to me preferable to that of humans had no taste for mine. I had to run after them, arm myself with patience, use trickery, imprison them in a matchbox or a jam jar, and the most majestic among them always evaded me owing to the contrast, the incompatibility, perhaps, between their size, beauty, rarity and my smallness, ugliness, mediocrity.

I retain memories of stinging disappointments, among grandpa's zinnias. I would be almost sure of having intercepted the Sparrow Sphinx, and cautiously unclenching my fingers, would realize that my hand was empty and that the insect kept fluttering as if nothing was the matter, contemptuous, ironic perhaps, right over the neighboring flower. I already no longer counted on the adults to be able to help me in any way, and kept to myself the reflections they inspired in me, namely that they were hopeless. Reality, with which they were making do, was essentially – they only had to look! – devoid of charm, of glow, of savor. One noted, nevertheless, in certain hours of the day and periods of the year, some interesting details, the Sparrow Sphinx but not only, some others, of which I'll speak later. Yet, these apparitions, these exceptions were evading me with an imperceptible beating of their wings. All that was left was some grey, some sadness mixed with disappointment, and one didn't care about it, around me.

We were not up to the task. There were more things in the world than we were putting in it. It wasn't just a maze of sad streets lined with bister-colored sandstone houses and prosaic occupations. It included margins, interstices haunted by colorful creatures which at first sight seemed uncatchable, but that it wasn't absolutely excluded we might catch if we used adequate means.

It wasn't on grandpa's zinnias that I eventually captured the Sphinx, and grandpa was no longer around for me to explain to him, with evidence at hand, what prodigy it constituted, this living little flame oscillating in the glass jar in which I had imprisoned it. But I was thinking of him. I was detailing, in my inner voice, the remarkable peculiarities of the creature of orangey wings beating so fast one couldn't see them. They made one think of a flame the insect would have been emitting continually, of a living, unquenchable fire. There was also that little feathery piebald tuft, as of a bird, and the disproportionate tongue, like a black wire, that it plunged into the flowers' calyx. It drew from it its erudite name, Macroglossum Stellatarum, which I would get still later in books where, against all expectations, it was discussed.

Running after insects, collecting rocks, reading continually, instead of acting, which seem insane past a certain age, are much less so and perhaps not at all if one admits that the past remains present at every moment and doesn't recede, doesn't pass unless it has found its completion. It is occasionally the case, and then we're quits, available for new, current tasks. But sometimes, and more often than not, in the beginning, our ignorance, our negligence prevent us from getting what is very manifestly intended, necessary, salutary for us. We won't be spared from disappointment, from sadness. But if we're incapable of intercepting the passing wonders, and if the adults can't see a thing, do nothing of value, we always have the recourse of entrusting the one we will perhaps have become in turn, later, with the care of making up for the damages and losses we endured from the start. From him to us, there exists an essential continuity, and that is time.

From the day I realized the world was not entirely devoid of appeal but "foiled my expectations and thwarted my will" *, I had to put off to problematic tomorrows the best of what I yearned for. I wouldn't have returned to the attack years later, with a net, a flask of ether for knocking out my prey, pins for nailing them in glass boxes, labels mentioning their erudite names - Iphiclides podalirius (the Iberian scarce), Leptinotarsa decemlineata (the Colorado beetle) ... - if we were getting our wish just like that. It was a bitter subject of meditations, this primal, deep disharmony between our views, our desires and the objects concerned. I didn't bring it up, because I could also see that these thoughts, these pretensions were mine only. Ten times, no, a hundred, I had tried to alert an adult about this or that singular, salient fact without getting anything but a heedless, purely formal assent or the vague funny face meaning that one really doesn't understand what the matter is, that one can't see a thing, and I was glad if it wasn't mingled with suspicion.

*: Karl Marx

The adult should have sensed we were touching upon the fundamental question, which is, everywhere and always, that of reality. It is the one that surfaces when two persons stand together and one of them detects something the other doesn't perceive. Who doesn't appreciate the infinite consequences of this small disharmony? He who can't see a thing where he is told there definitely is something should strive to extend his views to what exists independently from us and, reciprocally, he who sees something while he's being assured there is nothing is required to reappraise himself and proportionate his ideas with that only which is with us and of which they are meant to be, should be the true reflection. I'm still waiting for the day I'll see an adult not even see but only try, make the effort, and I know that, for my part, I have persisted in holding interesting, important, real the beasts, the rocks, the objects after having taken the trouble of questioning myself, of doubting.

I can understand that insects were subjected to an unfavorable prejudice. Some of them deserved it: the Colorado beetles particularly, pullulating in those days, with their reddish, repugnant larvas on the potato plants, the white pierids whose caterpillars, of a beautiful green, were gnawing at the cabbages, the hornets buzzing up to nightfall in the thick of the fig tree. But though a pest to us, they nonetheless exhibited interesting features, bright colors, rare motifs, danger indeed, all very much worthy of interest.

My dark, secret suppositions about the adults' world were not as unfounded as I was imagining and blaming myself for.

But there had to be some among them that were of the kind that, as children, we yearn to meet, that is to say who remembered having been children, curious, perplexed and wishing to know once and for all, to be cleansed of the incertitude all things inspire in us in the beginning, starting with the thing they consisted in themselves, and which persisted with its reservations and longing.

One of them held indeed the answer to the questions the Sparrow Sphinx, the great evasive swallowtails, the candid nonchalant pierids were wordlessly asking me. But he was long dead. Witness of his passage was but an illegible marble plaque, perched high up on the façade of a house facing the porch of Saint-Martin's collegiate church. It had first been affixed on the side of a building overlooking in part

Toulzac street, in part Civoire square, which was on this occasion and temporarily rechristened Latreille square, since such was his name. A ceremony had taken place on October 6, 1907 in the presence of officials and ecclesiastical dignitaries, but senator François Labrousse and representative Edouard Lachaud, of the Radical Left, "preferred going to the agricultural show in Beaulieu instead of celebrating the scholar from Brive", according to the Catholic paper La Croix de la Corrèze. Then, I don't know when, they reckoned it was a mistake and that our illustrious compatriot's native house stood some sixty yards from there, in front of the church. The plaque was discreetly unfastened and transferred to its current site, which is not that much more guaranteed to be the right one. Latreille was the natural child of the baron of Espagnac and his mother abandoned him at birth. Hence the obscurity still shrouding the latter. We didn't entirely lose out. Stripped of the honor of having sounded with the first wails of the Prince of entomology, as the Dane Fabricius dubbed Latreille, the building on Civoire square found itself marked, a hundred years later exactly, with a new plaque, this one in memory of the three Bouyssonie brothers, Amédée, Jean, both of them priests like Latreille, and the layman Paul, who did indeed and successively see the light of day there. They were the ones who, in 1908, had exhumed from a neighboring cave the just about complete skeleton of the first French

Neanderthal. Hardly had the anceſtor seen the light of day again, after forty-five thousand years, that he was taking the express train to Paris in the satchel of Marcellin Boule who locked him up once more, in a safe of the Museum.

But I digress. Pierre-André Latreille was sent to Paris to ſtudy at Cardinal Lemoine College, which had been hoſting bursary holders since the 14th century. He was ordained a prieſt, returned to our small homeland and devoted himself to entomology, for which, to my knowledge, he never said where he got the taſte from. His firſt work was about the Mutillinae, small hymenopterans whose looks are between the wasps' and the ants' and which, the only of their kind, or of their family rather, ſtridulate like the cicadas and the grasshoppers. Then, the Revolution broke out. As he had refused to swear allegiance to its Civilian Conſtitution, Latreille was arreſted in 1793, jailed in Bordeaux and ſentenced to be deported to Guiana. The old tub taking him to the penal colony with two hundred other wretched fanatics didn't get paſt the Cordouan lighthouse. It sank. There were no survivors, except Latreille. He had been occupying his sad leisure inventorying the fauna of his humid and closed quarters. A small beetle with russet thorax had retained his attention, the which didn't escape that of a Sans-Culotte keen on natural hiſtory who put him apart from the chain of convicts at the time of boarding. Latreille was to give the name of Necrobia – life out of death – to the critter that had saved him from drowning.

Aside from the itinerant marble plaque, his Natural History of the Coleoptera Insects of Europe, placed there by himself perhaps, was gathering dust on a shelf on the premises of the local learned society. But nobody, as far as I knew, ever consulted it nor did I ever see anyone lift his eyes towards the plaque set too high up on the façade of his alleged native house.

I was very precisely half a world away from imagining my disappointment was part of an overall plan whose effects I had immediately verified in grandpa's garden, at a man's eye, or a child's eye level. Not only did I not know the names, if they had any, of the winged visitors of the potatoes and zinnias, but grandpa, at the other end of time, was no wiser than me, nor was anyone to whom I talked about them before I brought myself to swallow the reflections and other crazy observations inspired in me by reality, or what I held as such. From my third or sixth year onwards – grandpa left us when I was seven – my philosophy of life was settled. The world was a mystery and denied itself to us, to our undertakings, to our thoughts. Its most beautiful specimens were evading us with an imperceptible beating of their wings, and we would never know anything more precise about them than their resemblance to an orangey little flame, than the precious and fleeting ocellated motifs their wings were historiated with.

How could I then conceive that, for reasons that were the last I had suspected, my disappointment was in the nature of things and would bind me to my last day?

A little over ten years later I left the cramped, enigmatic world I had received in endowment for the big city, whose first effect was to ruin the axiom drawn from the frequentation of insects, of adults. To say it in few words, reality was not in essence rebellious to our undertakings, forever impenetrable to our thoughts.

It was naturally not to let me indulge in childishnesses that I was dispatched afar, but it's all our past we bring along with us en route to the future, and in my boarder's trunk were the dispiriting philosophy my small homeland had inculcated me with, the questions that accompany us as long as they haven't been answered. I didn't go to the Museum immediately. There was serious business that had to be dealt with at once and, anyway, the institution, which was letting in water, was closed for repairs and for a long time. Then it reopened its doors. I went. The first thing I saw was Latreille's profile in low relief, on the façade, with his name perfectly legible below, and then the insects I had once chased without success, displayed behind glass, with their extraordinary forms, their incredible colors that could be contemplated indefinitely, their names.

We had the things at home, or some of them at least, but an occult, enemy power had placed the explanation afar and you had to lose the former to get the latter, or to content yourself with the one without ever having seen, touched (sometimes) the others. And perhaps – I don't know – it then lacked the vibration, the galvanic, irreplaceable contact which things impress in our thoughts, the appeal of life itself.

Though lifeless and motionless, the mineral realm was inducing no lesser perplexity and kept a similar muteness. It didn't even stridulate, like the Muttilinae.

It may well be that no other place on earth is as richly furnished in this respect as ours. Almost all of the geological system found itself concentrated within a quadrangle a few miles square. In the north, we were overlooked by the old Precambrian crystalline massif. In the opposite direction spread the deposits of the secondary seas. The lavas of neighboring Auvergne had overflowed upon the eastern edge of the county, while the levelled West, having recently risen above water (somewhat), already had a very distant flavor of the ocean.

That's not all. The tumultuous life of the planet had more or less reshuffled the cards, rearranged the picture. So, we had under our feet, before our eyes, too, because it had served as building stone, an ochre sandstone coming from the erosion of the granitic heights. The aftermath of the Alp's late uplift had compressed and metamorphized the eastern zone, caused tight folds discouraging one from frequenting those parts.

Luckily, unlike insects, stone doesn't confine itself to decorating or ravaging gardens. It's used to build houses and a good knowledge of it is indispensable. An abundant literature had been dedicated to it as early as the 19th century and there were people, albeit in small number, who took an interest in it, studied its nature, its origin, called it by its name. They met at a fixed time on Saturdays on the premises of the learned society, and even children and adolescents could open their door and submit to them questions they kindly listened to and answered when they could. One of them, a schoolmaster driven by a passion for learning and teaching, was willing to examine the contents of the boxes full of rocks and fossils that I submitted to his inspection at intervals. Among which, I remember, a fragment of light-colored stone I had taken, and so did he, for calcite, a soft rock. To check, he applied it on the lead-framed window glass, which he cracked from top to bottom. It was silica.

What I didn't know, because it belongs to a different science, to political economy, was that the rock explained just about everything, starting with the absence of explanation. And as no one cared much about it, it had an easy time limiting our views, darkening our lives, ruining hope.

Two very precise, very ancient memories remain with me. I had picked up an angular white rock in a sunken lane, on the hills surrounding town, and asked the old man accompanying me what it was. Answer: "flint". Now, I had already seen flint, in abundance, at the museum. The region abounded with prehistoric relics and the ground floor was furnished with display cases full of sharpened and polished axes, of chisels, of scrapers, of arrowheads whose brown hues and vitreous glow lent them no resemblance to the sort of sugar cube I had collected. But I was six or seven, my interlocutor ten times that, and I kept to myself my objection: "That's not it!" As for knowing what it was, the septuagenarian I would perhaps become would perhaps tell me.

Second memory: we paid a visit to some relatives who owned, among other curios, a meteorite whose mere name made you dream. Wow! This sphere about the size of a big orange, with its crested, grainy, rusty surface had travelled through the intergalactic spaces to land on a shelf in a living-dining room of our sub-prefecture! They put it in my hands. Its surprising density was that of iron. The feeling was to linger on for a long time. I would rejoice in secret at having had access, through the intercession of a meteorite, to the farthest reaches of the universe. Twenty years later, as I was working at answering the questions left unresolved ever since the origin, I discovered that the celestial body was nothing more than a scrap of marcasite, an iron disulphide of which the carbonated rocks of Chalky Champagne, of Brittany, of Pas-de-Calais are stuffed full.

The familiar universe was changing before our eyes every few miles, if not every hundred yards, which the feeling of existence, euphoric or miserable, was faithfully echoing. It was proof of the world's existence. The world prescribed us our moods, our thoughts, which were much more often sad than pleasant, and the reciprocal wasn't true. It refused to embrace the happy, easy dispositions into which we are spontaneously inclined to enter and remain. It opposed them with all its expanse, tenacity, permanence, deep and obscure antiquity.

One is reminded of the words of a German philosopher, a certain Hegel, herald of absolute idealism, upon discovering the Alps in the 1800s: "That is". A century and a half later, in the furrowed zone of mediocre elevation separating the Massif Central from the Aquitaine Basin, that also was, still, and the mind, puny as it was, like the landscape, was still bumping against it.

I would now and then leave the city, sitting in the backseat of a Renault 4CV whose engine, placed in the rear, covered with its sharp vindictive hum whatever words one might have wished to address to the driver. Anyway, I no longer expected any answer and kept quiet. I contented myself with recording the sudden alterations of outer reality whose physiognomy, depending on which direction we took, was changing as it ordinarily only does at large intervals, under other latitudes if not on other planets. Had I seen the light of day some distance away, in one of the four geological regions at whose crossroads we stood, I wouldn't have had to ask myself. The contrasts and contraries wouldn't have forced me to. I would have known, in this respect, a kind of equanimity of the soul, a little peace. But it was signed and sealed somewhere that they were to be denied me, and it was the earth in person that was opposing it.

I still wonder, at the other end of time, at the speed with which one scenery would chase away another. Hardly had my father pointed the car's round and hollow nose towards one of the cardinal points that I would undertake to bring myself into unison with those parts he was leading us to, since it was they, and not we, that were setting the tone. You had to guard yourself, as much as possible, against the primal, fundamental discord between within and without. It was so marked, in places, that I would see to it long in advance. It was only at the cost of a slow, exhausting preparation that I would adopt the dispositions required by the zone whose direction I had immediately understood we were taking.

Luckily, one can feel things. It's not necessary to have explicitly reflected upon them to deal with them, somehow or other. My father most often took to the south, the only horizon answering the obscure need we have for amenity, for clarity, for ease. Hardly had we come out of a narrow and deep valley of bister-colored sandstone walls incised with caves like sunken eye-sockets, that the road - Route 20 - was contorting itself to climb the ridge on which rose the village of Noailles, and everything was suddenly different. Some of the houses were made of the same greyish brown, pulverulent sad stone as the town we had just left. But the others were built out of the clear, compact rock that had succeeded it halfway up the escarpment. I could place their meeting point within an inch, and proof that an outer world exists which prescribes us our affections, our thoughts, is that a profuse mirth was instantly coming to me. It had arisen when my father had taken to the top of the street we lived in, thus to the south. But a doubt remained. Once there, he might turn right to rejoin Route 20, but also left, towards the east and Xaintrie territory, a rugged, hostile dark zone, on road 121 with its continual bends that made me nauseous.

We never pushed to the north, which announced itself immediately after the bridge on the river, with a steep slope they called La Pigeonnie, and then, up to Limoges and beyond, billowed and fell back the deep petrified swell of the ancient granitic massif. I barely have memory of one or two incursions westwards, in Périgord planted with walnut trees and lovely Renaissance manors and populated with geese herds.

If our little moment differed from all preceding ones, it's been in that the answer was not given us before the question was asked. It was understood since always that things were what they were. There was no need to ask oneself, to look any further, for something else. And then we did. I would have given everything to take hold of the Sparrow Sphinx, to have an adult tell me its real name and the grounds for its behavior – a night moth, like all Sphingidae, it fluttered in broad daylight and, on account of I know not what spell, always evaded me. And also, how come the landscape never stopped changing, off-putting (in the north, in the east), disappointing (in the west), open, luminous, exhilarating in the south, past the valley of cavernous walls. But the moment had not come. The eccentrics versed in the knowledge of insects were deceased, their native houses ill identified, their books buried under dust and oblivion, and you had to ferret out the rare adults seeking to understand the landscape's variegation that couldn't fail to affect you.

I was about to leave when I exhumed the ones, interrogated the others. But it was elsewhere, afar, that the explanation was exiled, since it was from there that came the concern and confusion to which was subjected reality, or what passes as such. They could have manifested themselves earlier or later. In the first case, our predecessors would have settled the accounts and all we would have had to do was listen to them. In the second, we wouldn't have had a thing to care about. We would have resembled them. But it's to us that it happened.

OF FISH AND GAME
AND BUTTERFLIES

LAYOUT BY RESSOUVENANCES
02600 CŒUVRES (FRANCE)
MARCH 2020.

Printed in France

Imprimé en France
FRHW011435150722
31464FR00002B/44